All … belong to a kind of poet… 'narrative verse'. This is just another way … 'poems whose main purpose is to tell a story'. So the …ms in this collection have been chosen because they tell excellent stories – exciting, mysterious, weird, fabulous or tragic stories. They are also probably the fifteen most famous narrative poems in the English language, representing the work of eleven master poets.

SAMUEL TAYLOR COLERIDGE (1772–1834) was born in Devon, the youngest son of a vicar. He was a brilliant classical scholar, but his first love was the life of the imagination, and he devoted himself to poetry and the ideals of fellow Romantics such as William Wordsworth and Robert Southey.

SIR WALTER SCOTT (1771–1832) is Scotland's second poet, after Robert Burns. Born in Edinburgh, he was always fascinated by Scottish history and legends, and much of his poetry draws on this rich background. In 1813 he was asked to become Poet Laureate, but he refused; in 1820, however, he accepted a baronetcy.

JOHN KEATS (1795–1821) was born in London, the son of a poor stableman, but as a teenager he discovered poetry. For the last two years of his tragically short life he was too ill to write, so all his poetry – which is recognized as some of the greatest ever written – was composed in three short years, between about 1816 and 1819. He died of tuberculosis.

ALFRED, LORD TENNYSON (1809–92) was the third son of the rector of Somersby, Lincolnshire. He began to have poetry published while he was a student at Cambridge University, and soon became the most popular poet of his time. He was made Poet Laureate in 1850 and the first Baron Tennyson in 1884.

RICHARD HARRIS BARHAM (1788–1845) was not primarily a poet, but a canon of St Paul's Cathedral. However, under the pseudonym of Thomas Ingoldsby, he began to publish the poems which formed *The Ingoldsby Legends*, whose lively rhythms and often comic treatment of medieval legends guaranteed the book's immediate and permanent popularity.

THOMAS BABINGTON MACAULAY, LORD MACAULAY (1800–59) was a historian, an essayist and a politician; for some years, in fact, he was a Whig Member of Parliament. All his writings, both poetry and prose, were immensely successful.

ROBERT BROWNING (1812–89) was born in Camberwell (now part of London), the son of a clerk in the Bank of England. In 1846, by which time he was a moderately famous poet, he eloped with the poetess Elizabeth Barrett to Italy, where he lived until she died in 1861. He returned to find enormous fame in London; indeed, the Browning Society was formed in 1881, during his lifetime!

EDGAR ALLAN POE (1809–49) was born in Boston, Massachusetts, the son of travelling actors. He was orphaned at an early age and his life is a tale of poverty and suffering. He refused regular employment, preferring to write, but although his poems and stories brought him fame, they did not make him rich, and he died a lonely alcoholic.

HENRY WADSWORTH LONGFELLOW (1807–82) was born in Portland, Maine. He travelled extensively in Europe and was fluent in several modern languages, which he taught, chiefly at the famous Harvard University, for many years. Even during his time as a professor, however, he was writing poetry, and for much of his life he was the best-loved poet in the United States.

MATTHEW ARNOLD (1822–88) was the eldest son of Thomas Arnold, the famous headmaster of Rugby School. His poetry was mostly written when he was quite young and from the 1860s onwards he became better known for his essays on literary, social and educational matters.

ROBERT LOUIS BALFOUR STEVENSON (1850–94) was born in Edinburgh. His parents wanted him to become a lawyer, but he had already decided to devote himself to writing. He is as famous for his novels (such as *Treasure Island*) as he is for his poetry.

The Rime of the Ancient Mariner and Other Classic Stories in Verse

SELECTED AND EDITED BY
ROBIN WATERFIELD

PUFFIN BOOKS

PUFFIN BOOKS

Published by the Penguin Group
Penguin Books Ltd, 27 Wrights Lane, London W8 5TZ, England
Penguin Books USA Inc., 375 Hudson Street, New York, New York 10014, USA
Penguin Books Australia Ltd, Ringwood, Victoria, Australia
Penguin Books Canada Ltd, 10 Alcorn Avenue, Toronto, Ontario, Canada M4V 3B2
Penguin Books (NZ) Ltd, 182–190 Wairau Road, Auckland 10, New Zealand

Penguin Books Ltd, Registered Offices: Harmondsworth, Middlesex, England

First published 1996
1 3 5 7 9 10 8 6 4 2

Filmset by Datix International Limited, Bungay, Suffolk
Printed in England by Clays Ltd, St Ives plc
Set in 10/14pt Monotype Plantin

CONTENTS

The Rime of the Ancient Mariner

Samuel Taylor Coleridge

This version first published in *Sibylline Leaves* (1817)

PART I

An ancient Mariner meeteth three Gallants bidden to a wedding-feast, and detaineth one.

It is an ancient Mariner
And he stoppeth one of three.
'By thy long grey beard and glittering eye,
Now wherefore stopp'st thou me?

The Bridegroom's doors are opened wide,
And I am next of kin;
The guests are met, the feast is set:
Mayst hear the merry din.'

He holds him with his skinny hand,
'There was a ship,' quoth he.
'Hold off! unhand me, grey-beard loon!'
Eftsoons his hand dropt he.

The Wedding-Guest is spellbound by the eye of the old seafaring man, and constrained to hear his tale.

He holds him with his glittering eye –
The Wedding-Guest stood still,
And listens like a three years' child:
The Mariner hath his will.

The Wedding-Guest sat on a stone:
He cannot choose but hear;
And thus spake on that ancient man,
The bright-eyed Mariner.

The Mariner tells how the ship sailed southward with a good wind and fair weather, till it reached the Line.

The ship was cheered, the harbour cleared,
Merrily did we drop
Below the kirk, below the hill,
Below the lighthouse top.

The Sun came up upon the left,
Out of the sea came he!
And he shone bright, and on the right
Went down into the sea.

Higher and higher every day,
Till over the mast at noon –'
The Wedding-Guest here beat his breast,
For he heard the loud bassoon.

The Wedding-Guest heareth the bridal music; but the Mariner continueth his tale.

The bride hath paced into the hall,
Red as a rose is she;
Nodding their heads before her goes
The merry minstrelsy.

The Wedding-Guest he beat his breast,
Yet he cannot choose but hear;
And thus spake on that ancient man,
The bright-eyed Mariner.

The ship driven by a storm toward the South Pole.

'And now the STORM-BLAST came, and he
Was tyrannous and strong:
He struck with his o'ertaking wings,
And chased us south along.

With sloping masts and dipping prow,
As who pursued with yell and blow
Still treads the shadow of his foe,
And forward bends his head,
The ship drove fast, loud roared the blast,
And southward aye we fled.

And now there came both mist and snow,
And it grew wondrous cold:
And ice, mast-high, came floating by,
As green as emerald.

The land of ice, and of fearful sounds where no living thing was to be seen.

And through the drifts the snowy clifts
Did send a dismal sheen:
Nor shapes of men nor beasts we ken –
The ice was all between.

The ice was here, the ice was there,
The ice was all around:
It cracked and growled, and roared and howled,
Like noises in a swound!

Till a great sea-bird, called the Albatross, came through the snow-fog, and was received with great joy and hospitality.

At length did cross an Albatross,
Thorough the fog it came;
As if it had been a Christian soul,
We hailed it in God's name.

It ate the food it ne'er had eat,
And round and round it flew.
The ice did split with a thunder-fit;
The helmsman steered us through!

And lo! the Albatross proveth a bird of good omen, and followeth the ship as it returned northward through fog and floating ice.

And a good south wind sprung up behind;
The Albatross did follow,
And every day, for food or play,
Came to the mariner's hollo!

In mist or cloud, on mast or shroud,
It perched for vespers nine;
Whiles all the night, through fog-smoke white,
Glimmered the white Moon-shine.'

The ancient Mariner inhospitably killeth the pious bird of good omen.

'God save thee, ancient Mariner!
From the fiends, that plague thee thus! –
Why look'st thou so?' – 'With my cross-bow
I shot the ALBATROSS.'

PART II

'The Sun now rose upon the right:
Out of the sea came he,
Still hid in mist, and on the left
Went down into the sea.

And the good south wind still blew behind,
But no sweet bird did follow,
Nor any day for food or play
Came to the mariners' hollo!

His shipmates cry out against the ancient Mariner, for killing the bird of good luck.

And I had done a hellish thing,
And it would work 'em woe:
For all averred, I had killed the bird
That made the breeze to blow.
Ah wretch! said they, the bird to slay,
That made the breeze to blow!

But when the fog cleared off, they justify the same, and thus make themselves accomplices in the crime.

Nor dim nor red, like God's own head,
The glorious Sun uprist:
Then all averred, I had killed the bird
That brought the fog and mist.
'Twas right, said they, such birds to slay,
That bring the fog and mist.

The fair breeze continues: the ship enters the Pacific Ocean, and sails northward, even till it reaches the Line.

The fair breeze blew, the white foam flew,
The furrow followed free;
We were the first that ever burst
Into that silent sea.

Down dropt the breeze, the sails dropt down,
'Twas sad as sad could be;
And we did speak only to break
The silence of the sea!

The ship hath been suddenly becalmed.

All in a hot and copper sky,
The bloody Sun, at noon,
Right up above the mast did stand,
No bigger than the Moon.

Day after day, day after day,
We stuck, nor breath nor motion;
As idle as a painted ship
Upon a painted ocean.

And the Albatross begins to be avenged.

Water, water, everywhere,
And all the boards did shrink;
Water, water, everywhere,
Nor any drop to drink.

The very deep did rot: O Christ!
That ever this should be!
Yea, slimy things did crawl with legs
Upon the slimy sea.

About, about, in reel and rout
The death-fires danced at night;
The water, like a witch's oils,
Burnt green, and blue and white.

A Spirit had followed them; one of the invisible inhabitants of this planet, neither departed souls nor angels; concerning whom the learned Jew, Josephus, and the Platonic Constantinopolitan, Michael Psellus, may be consulted. They are very numerous, and there is no climate or element without one or more.

And some in dreams assurèd were
Of the Spirit that plagued us so;
Nine fathom deep he had followed us
From the land of mist and snow.

And every tongue, through utter drought,
Was withered at the root;
We could not speak, no more than if
We had been choked with soot.

The shipmates in their sore distress, would fain throw the whole guilt on the ancient Mariner: in sign whereof they hang the dead seabird round his neck.

Ah! well a-day! What evil looks
Had I from old and young!
Instead of the cross, the Albatross
About my neck was hung.'

PART III

'There passed a weary time. Each throat
Was parched, and glazed each eye.
A weary time! a weary time!
How glazed each weary eye,

The ancient Mariner beholdeth a sign in the element afar off.

When looking westward, I beheld
A something in the sky.

At first it seemed a little speck,
And then it seemed a mist;
It moved and moved, and took at last
A certain shape, I wist.

A speck, a mist, a shape, I wist!
And still it neared and neared:
As if it dodged a water-sprite,
It plunged and tacked and veered.

At its nearer approach, it seemeth him to be a ship; and at a dear ransom he freeth his speech from the bonds of thirst.

With throats unslaked, with black lips baked,
We could nor laugh nor wail;
Through utter drought all dumb we stood!
I bit my arm, I sucked the blood,
And cried, A sail! a sail!

With throats unslaked, with black lips baked,
Agape they heard me call:

A flash of joy;

Gramercy! they for joy did grin,
And all at once their breath drew in,
As they were drinking all.

And horror follows. For can it be a ship that comes onward without wind or tide?

"See! see!" (I cried) "she tacks no more!
Hither to work us weal;
Without a breeze, without a tide,
She steadies with upright keel!"

The western wave was all a-flame.
The day was well nigh done!
Almost upon the western wave
Rested the broad bright Sun;
When that strange shape drove suddenly
Betwixt us and the Sun.

It seemeth him but the skeleton of a ship.

And straight the Sun was flecked with bars,
(Heaven's Mother send us grace!)
As if through a dungeon-grate he peered
With broad and burning face.

Alas! (thought I, and my heart beat loud)
How fast she nears and nears!
Are those *her* sails that glance in the Sun,
Like restless gossameres?

And its ribs are seen as bars on the face of the setting Sun. The Spectre-Woman and her Death-mate, and no other on board the skeleton ship.

Are those *her* ribs through which the Sun
Did peer, as through a grate?
And is that Woman all her crew?
Is that a DEATH? and are there two?
Is DEATH that woman's mate?

Like vessel, like crew! Death and Life-in-Death have diced for the ship's crew, and she (the latter) winneth the ancient Mariner.

Her lips were red, *her* looks were free,
Her locks were yellow as gold:
Her skin was as white as leprosy,
The Night-mare LIFE-IN-DEATH was she,
Who thicks man's blood with cold.

The naked hulk alongside came,
And the twain were casting dice;
"The game is done! I've won! I've won!"
Quoth she, and whistles thrice.

No twilight within the courts of the Sun.

The Sun's rim dips; the stars rush out:
At one stride comes the dark;
With far-heard whisper, o'er the sea,
Off shot the spectre-bark.

At the rising of the Moon,

We listened and looked sideways up!
Fear at my heart, as at a cup,
My life-blood seemed to sip!
The stars were dim, and thick the night,
The steersman's face by his lamp gleamed white;
From the sails the dew did drip –
Till clomb above the eastern bar
The hornèd Moon, with one bright star
Within the nether tip.

One after another,

One after one, by the star-dogged Moon,
Too quick for groan or sigh,
Each turned his face with a ghastly pang,
And cursed me with his eye.

His shipmates drop down dead.

Four times fifty living men,
(And I heard nor sigh nor groan)
With heavy thump, a lifeless lump,
They dropped down one by one.

But Life-in-Death begins her work on the ancient Mariner.

The souls did from their bodies fly –
They fled to bliss or woe!
And every soul, it passed me by,
Like the whizz of my cross-bow!'

PART IV

The Wedding-Guest feareth that a Spirit is talking to him;

'I fear thee, ancient Mariner!
I fear thy skinny hand!
And thou art long, and lank, and brown,
As is the ribbed sea-sand.

I fear thee and thy glittering eye,
And thy skinny hand, so brown.' –
'Fear not, fear not, thou Wedding-Guest!
This body dropt not down.

But the ancient Mariner assureth him of his bodily life, and proceedeth to relate his horrible penance.

Alone, alone, all, all alone,
Alone on a wide wide sea!
And never a saint took pity on
My soul in agony.

he despiseth the creatures of the calm,

The many men, so beautiful!
And they all dead did lie:
And a thousand thousand slimy things
Lived on; and so did I.

And envieth that *they* should live, and so many lie dead.

I looked upon the rotting sea,
And drew my eyes away;
I looked upon the rotting deck,
And there the dead men lay.

I looked to Heaven, and tried to pray;
But or ever a prayer had gusht,
A wicked whisper came, and made
My heart as dry as dust.

I closed my lids, and kept them close,
And the balls like pulses beat;
For the sky and the sea, and the sea and the sky
Lay like a load on my weary eye,
And the dead were at my feet.

But the curse liveth for him in the eye of the dead men.

The cold sweat melted from their limbs,
Nor rot nor reek did they:
The look with which they looked on me
Had never passed away.

An orphan's curse would drag to hell
A spirit from on high;
But oh! more horrible than that
Is the curse in a dead man's eye!
Seven days, seven nights, I saw that curse,
And yet I could not die.

In his loneliness and fixedness he yearneth towards the journeying Moon, and the stars that still sojourn, yet still move onward; and everywhere the blue sky belongs to them, and is their appointed rest, and their native country and their own natural homes, which they enter unannounced, as lords that are certainly expected and yet there is a silent joy at their arrival.

The moving Moon went up the sky,
And nowhere did abide:
Softly she was going up,
And a star or two beside –

Her beams bemocked the sultry main,
Like April hoar-frost spread;
But where the ship's huge shadow lay,
The charmèd water burnt alway
A still and awful red.

By the light of the Moon he beholdeth God's creatures of the great calm.

Beyond the shadow of the ship,
I watched the water-snakes:
They moved in tracks of shining white,
And when they reared, the elfish light
Fell off in hoary flakes.

Within the shadow of the ship
I watched their rich attire:
Blue, glossy green, and velvet black,
They coiled and swam; and every track
Was a flash of golden fire.

Their beauty and their happiness.

O happy living things! no tongue
Their beauty might declare:
A spring of love gushed from my heart,
And I blessed them unaware:
Sure my kind saint took pity on me,
And I blessed them unaware.

He blesseth them in his heart.

The self-same moment I could pray;
And from my neck so free
The Albatross fell off, and sank
Like lead into the sea.'

The spell begins to break.

PART V

'Oh sleep! it is a gentle thing,
Beloved from pole to pole!
To Mary Queen the praise be given!
She sent the gentle sleep from Heaven,
That slid into my soul.

By grace of the holy Mother, the ancient Mariner is refreshed with rain.

The silly buckets on the deck,
That had so long remained,
I dreamt that they were filled with dew;
And when I awoke, it rained.

My lips were wet, my throat was cold,
My garments all were dank;
Sure I had drunken in my dreams,
And still my body drank.

I moved, and could not feel my limbs:
I was so light – almost
I thought that I had died in sleep,
And was a blessèd ghost.

He heareth sounds and seeth strange sights and commotions in the sky and the element.

And soon I heard a roaring wind:
It did not come anear;
But with its sound it shook the sails,
That were so thin and sere.

The upper air burst into life!
And a hundred fire-flags sheen,
To and fro they were hurried about!
And to and fro, and in and out,
The wan stars danced between.

And the coming wind did roar more loud,
And the sails did sigh like sedge;
And the rain poured down from one black cloud;
The Moon was at its edge.

The thick black cloud was cleft, and still
The Moon was at its side:
Like waters shot from some high crag,
The lightning fell with never a jag,
A river steep and wide.

The bodies of the ship's crew are inspired, and the ship moves on;

The loud wind never reached the ship,
Yet now the ship moved on!
Beneath the lightning and the Moon
The dead men gave a groan.

They groaned, they stirred, they all uprose,
Nor spake, nor moved their eyes;
It had been strange, even in a dream,
To have seen those dead men rise.

The helmsman steered, the ship moved on;
Yet never a breeze up-blew;
The mariners all 'gan work the ropes,
Where they were wont to do;
They raised their limbs like lifeless tools –
We were a ghastly crew.

The body of my brother's son
Stood by me, knee to knee:
The body and I pulled at one rope,
But he said nought to me.'

'I fear thee, ancient Mariner!'
'Be calm, thou Wedding-Guest!
'Twas not those souls that fled in pain,
Which to their corses came again,
But a troop of spirits blest:

But not by the souls of the men, nor by daemons of earth or middle air, but by a blessed troop of angelic spirits, sent down by the invocation of the guardian saint.

For when it dawned – they dropped their arms,
And clustered round the mast;
Sweet sounds rose slowly through their mouths,
And from their bodies passed.

Around, around, flew each sweet sound,
Then darted to the Sun;
Slowly the sounds came back again,
Now mixed, now one by one.

Sometimes a-dropping from the sky
I heard the sky-lark sing;
Sometimes all little birds that are,
How they seemed to fill the sea and air
With their sweet jargoning!

And now 'twas like all instruments,
Now like a lonely flute;
And now it is an angel's song,
That makes the heavens be mute.

It ceased; yet still the sails made on
A pleasant noise till noon,
A noise like of a hidden brook
In the leafy month of June,
That to the sleeping woods all night
Singeth a quiet tune.

Till noon we quietly sailed on,
Yet never a breeze did breathe:
Slowly and smoothly went the ship,
Moved onward from beneath.

The lonesome Spirit from the South Pole carries on the ship as far as the Line, in obedience to the angelic troop, but still requireth vengeance.

Under the keel nine fathom deep,
From the land of mist and snow,
The spirit slid: and it was he
That made the ship to go.
The sails at noon left off their tune,
And the ship stood still also.

The Sun, right up above the mast,
Had fixed her to the ocean:
But in a minute she 'gan stir,
With a short uneasy motion –
Backwards and forwards half her length
With a short uneasy motion.

Then like a pawing horse let go,
She made a sudden bound:
It flung the blood into my head,
And I fell down in a swound.

The Polar Spirit's fellow-daemons, the invisible inhabitants of the element, take part in his wrong; and two of them relate, one to the other, that penance long and heavy for the ancient Mariner hath been accorded to the Polar Spirit who returneth southward.

How long in that same fit I lay,
I have not to declare;
But ere my living life returned,
I heard and in my soul discerned
Two voices in the air.

"Is it he?" quoth one, "Is this the man?
By him who died on cross,
With his cruel bow he laid full low
The harmless Albatross.

The spirit who bideth by himself
In the land of mist and snow,
He loved the bird that loved the man
Who shot him with his bow."

The other was a softer voice,
As soft as honey-dew:
Quoth he, "The man hath penance done,
And penance more will do."'

PART VI

FIRST VOICE

'"But tell me, tell me! speak again,
Thy soft response renewing –
What makes that ship drive on so fast?
What is the ocean doing?"

SECOND VOICE

"Still as a slave before his lord,
The ocean hath no blast;
His great bright eye most silently
Up to the Moon is cast –

If he may know which way to go;
For she guides him smooth or grim.
See, brother, see! how graciously
She looketh down on him."

FIRST VOICE

The Mariner hath been cast into a trance; for the angelic power causeth the vessel to drive northward faster than human life could endure.

"But why drives on that ship so fast,
Without or wave or wind?"

SECOND VOICE

"The air is cut away before,
And closes from behind.

Fly, brother, fly! more high, more high!
Or we shall be belated:
For slow and slow that ship will go,
When the Mariner's trance is abated."

The supernatural motion is retarded; the Mariner awakes, and his penance begins anew.

I woke, and we were sailing on
As in a gentle weather:
'Twas night, calm night, the moon was high;
The dead men stood together.

All stood together on the deck,
For a charnel-dungeon fitter:
All fixed on me their stony eyes,
That in the Moon did glitter.

The pang, the curse, with which they died,
Had never passed away:
I could not draw my eyes from theirs,
Nor turn them up to pray.

The curse is finally expiated.

And now this spell was snapt: once more
I viewed the ocean green,
And looked far forth, yet little saw
Of what had else been seen –

Like one, that on a lonesome road
Doth walk in fear and dread,
And having once turned round walks on,
And turns no more his head;
Because he knows, a frightful fiend
Doth close behind him tread.

But soon there breathed a wind on me,
Nor sound nor motion made:
Its path was not upon the sea,
In ripple or in shade.

It raised my hair, it fanned my cheek
Like a meadow-gale of spring –
It mingled strangely with my fears,
Yet it felt like a welcoming.

Swiftly, swiftly flew the ship,
Yet she sailed softly too:
Sweetly, sweetly blew the breeze –
On me alone it blew.

And the ancient Mariner beholdeth his native country.

Oh! dream of joy! is this indeed
The lighthouse top I see?
Is this the hill? is this the kirk?
Is this mine own countree?

We drifted o'er the harbour-bar,
And I with sobs did pray –
O let me be awake, my God!
Or let me sleep alway.

The harbour-bay was clear as glass,
So smoothly it was strewn!
And on the bay the moonlight lay,
And the shadow of the Moon.

The rock shone bright, the kirk no less,
That stands above the rock:
The moonlight steeped in silentness
The steady weathercock.

And the bay was white with silent light,
Till rising from the same,
Full many shapes, that shadows were:
In crimson colours came.

The angelic spirits leave the dead bodies,

A little distance from the prow
Those crimson shadows were:
I turned my eyes upon the deck –
Oh, Christ! what saw I there!

And appear in their own forms of light.

Each corse lay flat, lifeless and flat,
And, by the holy rood!
A man all light, a seraph-man,
On every corse there stood.

This seraph-band, each waved his hand:
It was a heavenly sight!
They stood as signals to the land,
Each one a lovely light;

This seraph-band, each waved his hand,
No voice did they impart –
No voice; but oh! the silence sank
Like music on my heart.

But soon I heard the dash of oars,
I heard the Pilot's cheer;
My head was turned perforce away
And I saw a boat appear.

The Pilot and the Pilot's boy,
I heard them coming fast:
Dear Lord in Heaven! it was a joy
The dead men could not blast.

I saw a third – I heard his voice:
It is the Hermit good!
He singeth loud his godly hymns
That he makes in the wood.
He'll shrieve my soul, he'll wash away
The Albatross's blood.

PART VII

The Hermit of the Wood,

This Hermit good lives in that wood
Which slopes down to the sea.
How loudly his sweet voice he rears!
He loves to talk with marineres
That come from a far countree.

He kneels at morn, and noon, and eve –
He hath a cushion plump:
It is the moss that wholly hides
The rotted old oak-stump.

The skiff-boat neared: I heard them talk,
"Why, this is strange, I trow!
Where are those lights so many and fair,
That signal made but now?"

Approacheth the ship with wonder.

"Strange, by my faith!" the Hermit said –
"And they answered not our cheer!
The planks look warped! and see those sails,
How thin they are and sere!
I never saw aught like to them,
Unless perchance it were

Brown skeletons of leaves that lag
My forest-brook along;
When the ivy-tod is heavy with snow,
And the owlet whoops to the wolf below,
That eats the she-wolf's young."

"Dear Lord! it hath a fiendish look –"
(The Pilot made reply)
"I am a-feared" – "Push on, push on!"
Said the Hermit cheerily.

The boat came closer to the ship,
But I nor spake nor stirred;
The boat came close beneath the ship,
And straight a sound was heard.

The ship suddenly sinketh.

Under the water it rumbled on,
Still louder and more dread:
It reached the ship, it split the bay;
The ship went down like lead.

The ancient Mariner is saved in the Pilot's boat.

Stunned by that loud and dreadful sound,
Which sky and ocean smote,
Like one that hath been seven days drowned
My body lay afloat;
But swift as dreams, myself I found
Within the Pilot's boat.

Upon the whirl, where sank the ship,
The boat spun round and round;
And all was still, save that the hill
Was telling of the sound.

I moved my lips – the Pilot shrieked
And fell down in a fit;
The holy Hermit raised his eyes,
And prayed where he did sit.

I took the oars: the Pilot's boy,
Who now doth crazy go,
Laughed loud and long, and all the while
His eyes went to and fro.
"Ha! Ha!" quoth he, "full plain I see,
The Devil knows how to row."

And now, all in my own countree,
I stood on the firm land!
The Hermit stepped forth from the boat,
And scarcely he could stand.

The ancient Mariner earnestly entreateth the Hermit to shrieve him; and the penance of life falls on him.

"O shrieve me, shrieve me, holy man!"
The Hermit crossed his brow.
"Say quick," quoth he, "I bid thee say –
What manner of man art thou?"

Forthwith this frame of mine was wrenched
With a woeful agony,
Which forced me to begin my tale;
And then it left me free.

And ever and anon throughout his future life an agony constraineth him to travel from land to land;

Since then, at an uncertain hour,
That agony returns:
And till my ghastly tale is told,
This heart within me burns.

I pass, like night, from land to land;
I have strange power of speech;
That moment that his face I see,
I know the man that must hear me:
To him my tale I teach.

What loud uproar bursts from that door!
The wedding-guests are there:
But in the garden-bower the bride
And bride-maids singing are:
And hark the little vesper bell,
Which biddeth me to prayer!

O Wedding-Guest! this soul hath been
Along on a wide wide sea:
So lonely 'twas, that God himself
Scarce seemed there to be.

O sweeter than the marriage-feast,
'Tis sweeter far to me,
To walk together to the kirk
With a goodly company! –

To walk together to the kirk,
And all together pray,
While each to his great Father bends,
Old men, and babes, and loving friends
And youths and maiden gay!

And to teach, by his own example, love and reverence to all things that God made and loveth.

Farewell, farewell! but this I tell
To thee, thou Wedding-Guest!
He prayeth well, who loveth well
Both man and bird and beast.

He prayeth best, who loveth best
All things both great and small;
For the dear God who loveth us,
He made and loveth all.'

The Mariner, whose eye is bright,
Whose beard with age is hoar,
Is gone: and now the Wedding-Guest
Turned from the bridegroom's door.

He went like one that hath been stunned,
And is of sense forlorn:
A sadder and a wiser man,
He rose the morrow morn.

Kubla Khan

Samuel Taylor Coleridge

An unfinished poem composed in 1797 and first published in *Christabel and Other Poems* (1816)

In Xanadu did Kubla Khan
A stately pleasure-dome decree:
Where Alph, the sacred river, ran
Through caverns measureless to man
  Down to a sunless sea.
So twice five miles of fertile ground
With walls and towers were girdled round:
And there were gardens bright with sinuous rills
Where blossom'd many an incense-bearing tree;
And here were forests ancient as the hills,
Enfolding sunny spots of greenery.

But O, that deep romantic chasm which slanted
Down the green hill athwart a cedarn cover!
A savage place! as holy and enchanted
As e'er beneath a waning moon was haunted
By woman wailing for her demon-lover!
And from this chasm, with ceaseless turmoil seething,
As if this earth in fast thick pants were breathing,
A mighty fountain momently was forced;
Amid whose swift half-intermitted burst
Huge fragments vaulted like rebounding hail,
Or chaffy grain beneath the thresher's flail:
And 'mid these dancing rocks at once and ever

It flung up momently the sacred river.
Five miles meandering with a mazy motion
Through wood and dale the sacred river ran,
Then reach'd the caverns measureless to man,
And sank in tumult to a lifeless ocean:
And 'mid this tumult Kubla heard from far
Ancestral voices prophesying war!

The shadow of the dome of pleasure
Floated midway on the waves;
Where was heard the mingled measure
From the fountain and the caves.
It was a miracle of rare device,
A sunny pleasure-dome with caves of ice!

A damsel with a dulcimer
In a vision once I saw:
It was an Abyssinian maid,
And on her dulcimer she play'd,
Singing of Mount Abora.
Could I revive within me,
Her symphony and song,
To such a deep delight 'twould win me,
That with music loud and long,
I would build that dome in air,
That sunny dome! those caves of ice!
And all who heard should see them there,
And all should cry, Beware! Beware!
His flashing eyes, his floating hair!
Weave a circle round him thrice,
And close your eyes with holy dread,
For he on honey-dew hath fed,
And drunk the milk of Paradise.

Young Lochinvar

Sir Walter Scott

This version first published in *Marmion: A Tale of Flodden Field* (1808)

O, YOUNG Lochinvar is come out of the west,
Through all the wide Border his steed was the best;
And save his good broadsword he weapons had none,
He rode all unarmed, and he rode all alone.
So faithful in love, and so dauntless in war,
There never was knight like the young Lochinvar.

He stayed not for brake, and he stopped not for stone,
He swam the Esk river where ford there was none;
But ere he alighted at Netherby gate,
The bride had consented, the gallant came late:
For a laggard in love, and a dastard in war,
Was to wed the fair Ellen of brave Lochinvar.

So boldly he entered the Netherby Hall,
Among bridesmen, and kinsmen, and brothers, and all:
Then spoke the bride's father, his hand on his sword
(For the poor craven bridegroom said never a word),
'O come ye in peace here, or come ye in war,
Or to dance at our bridal, young Lord Lochinvar?'

'I long wooed your daughter, my suit you denied –
Love swells like the Solway, but ebbs like its tide –
And now am I come, with this lost love of mine,

To lead but one measure, drink one cup of wine.
There are maidens in Scotland more lovely by far,
That would gladly be bride to the young Lochinvar.'

The bride kissed the goblet: the knight took it up,
He quaffed off the wine, and he threw down the cup.
She looked down to blush, and she looked up to sigh,
With a smile on her lips, and a tear in her eye.
He took her soft hand, ere her mother could bar –
'Now tread we a measure!' said young Lochinvar.

So stately his form, and so lovely her face,
That never a hall such a galliard did grace;
While her mother did fret, and her father did fume,
And the bridegroom stood dangling his bonnet and plume;
And the bride-maidens whispered, ''Twere better by far,
To have matched our fair cousin with young Lochinvar.'

One touch to her hand, and one word in her ear,
When they reached the hall door, and the charger stood near;
So light to the croupe the fair lady he swung,
So light to the saddle before her he sprung!
'She is won! we are gone, over bank, bush, and scaur;
They'll have fleet steeds that follow,' quoth young Lochinvar.

There was mounting 'mong Graemes of the Netherby clan;
Forsters, Fenwicks, and Musgraves, they rode and they ran:
There was racing and chasing on Cannobie Lee,
But the lost bride of Netherby ne'er did they see.
So daring in love, and so dauntless in war,
Have ye e'er heard of gallant like young Lochinvar?

The Eve of St. Agnes

John Keats

First published in *Lamia, Isabella, The Eve of St. Agnes and Other Poems* (1820)

St. Agnes' Eve – Ah, bitter chill it was!
The owl, for all his feathers, was a-cold;
The hare limped trembling through the frozen grass,
And silent was the flock in woolly fold:
Numb were the Beadsman's fingers, while he told
His rosary, and while his frosted breath,
Like pious incense from a censer old,
Seemed taking flight for heaven, without a death,
Past the sweet Virgin's picture while his prayer he saith.

His prayer he saith, this patient, holy man;
Then takes his lamp, and riseth from his knees,
And back returneth, meagre, barefoot, wan,
Along the chapel aisle by slow degrees:
The sculptured dead, on each side, seem to freeze,
Emprisoned in black, purgatorial rails:
Knights, ladies, praying in dumb oratories,
He passeth by; and his weak spirit fails
To think how they may ache in icy hoods and mails.

Northward he turneth through a little door,
And scarce three steps, ere Music's golden tongue
Flattered to tears this aged man and poor;
But no – already had his deathbell rung;
The joys of all his life were said and sung:
His was harsh penance on St. Agnes' Eve:
Another way he went, and soon among
Rough ashes sat he for his soul's reprieve,
And all night kept awake, for sinners' sake to grieve.

That ancient Beadsman heard the prelude soft;
And so it chanced, for many a door was wide,
From hurry to and fro. Soon, up aloft,
The silver, snarling trumpets 'gan to chide:
The level chambers, ready with their pride,
Were glowing to receive a thousand guests:
The carved angels, ever eager-eyed,
Stared, where upon their heads the cornice rests,
With hair blown back, and wings put crosswise on their breasts.

At length burst in the argent revelry,
With plume, tiara, and all rich array,
Numerous as shadows haunting fairily
The brain, new stuffed, in youth, with triumphs gay
Of old romance. These let us wish away,
And turn, sole-thoughted, to one Lady there,
Whose heart had brooded, all that wintry day,
On love, and winged St. Agnes' saintly care,
As she had heard old dames full many times declare.

They told her how, upon St. Agnes' Eve,
Young virgins might have visions of delight,
And soft adorings from their loves receive
Upon the honeyed middle of the night,
If ceremonies due they did aright;
As, supperless to bed they must retire,
And couch supine their beauties, lily white;
Nor look behind, nor sideways, but require
Of Heaven with upward eyes for all that they desire.

Full of this whim was thoughtful Madeline:
The music, yearning like a God in pain,
She scarcely heard: her maiden eyes divine,
Fixed on the floor, saw many a sweeping train
Pass by – she heeded not at all: in vain
Came many a tiptoe, amorous cavalier,
And back retired; not cooled by high disdain,
But she saw not: her heart was otherwhere:
She sighed for Agnes' dreams, the sweetest of the year.

She danced along with vague, regardless eyes,
Anxious her lips, her breathing quick and short:
The hallowed hour was near at hand: she sighs
Amid the timbrels, and the thronged resort
Of whisperers in anger, or in sport;
'Mid looks of love, defiance, hate, and scorn,
Hoodwinked with faery fancy; all amort,
Save to St. Agnes and her lambs unshorn,
And all the bliss to be before tomorrow morn.

So, purposing each moment to retire,
She lingered still. Meantime, across the moors,
Had come young Porphyro, with heart on fire
For Madeline. Beside the portal doors,
Buttressed from moonlight, stands he, and implores
All saints to give him sight of Madeline,
But for one moment in the tedious hours,
That he might gaze and worship all unseen;
Perchance speak, kneel, touch, kiss – in sooth such things have been.

He ventures in: let no buzzed whisper tell:
All eyes be muffled, or a hundred swords
Will storm his heart, Love's fev'rous citadel:
For him, those chambers held barbarian hordes,
Hyena foemen, and hot-blooded lords,
Whose very dogs would execrations howl
Against his lineage: not one breast affords
Him any mercy, in that mansion foul,
Save one old beldame, weak in body and in soul.

Ah, happy chance! the aged creature came,
Shuffling along with ivory-headed wand,
To where he stood, hid from the torch's flame,
Behind a broad hall-pillar, far beyond
The sound of merriment and chorus bland:
He startled her; but soon she knew his face,
And grasped his fingers in her palsied hand,
Saying, 'Mercy, Porphyro! hie thee from this place:
They are all here tonight, the whole bloodthirsty race!

'Get hence! get hence! there's dwarfish Hildebrand;
He had a fever late, and in the fit
He cursed thee and thine, both house and land:
Then there's that old Lord Maurice, not a whit
More tame for his gray hairs – Alas me! flit!
Flit like a ghost away.' 'Ah, Gossip dear,
We're safe enough; here in this armchair sit,
And tell me how –' 'Good Saints! not here, not here;
Follow me, child, or else these stones will be thy bier.'

He followed through a lowly arched way,
Brushing the cobwebs with his lofty plume,
And as she muttered 'Well-a – well-a-day!'
He found him in a little moonlight room,
Pale, latticed, chill, and silent as a tomb.
'Now tell me where is Madeline,' said he,
'O tell me, Angela, by the holy loom
Which none but secret sisterhood may see,
When they St. Agnes' wool are weaving piously.'

'St. Agnes! Ah! it is St. Agnes' Eve –
Yet men will murder upon holy days:
Thou must hold water in a witch's sieve,
And be liege-lord of all the elves and fays,
To venture so: it fills me with amaze
To see thee, Porphyro! – St. Agnes' Eve!
God's help! my lady fair the conjuror plays
This very night: good angels her deceive!
But let me laugh awhile, I've mickle time to grieve.'

Feebly she laugheth in the languid moon,
While Porphyro upon her face doth look,
Like puzzled urchin on an aged crone
Who keepeth closed a wondrous riddle book,
As spectacled she sits in chimney nook.
But soon his eyes grew brilliant, when she told
His lady's purpose; and he scarce could brook
Tears, at the thought of those enchantments cold,
And Madeline asleep in lap of legends old.

Sudden a thought came like a full-blown rose,
Flushing his brow, and in his pained heart
Made purple riot: then doth he propose
A stratagem, that makes the beldame start:
'A cruel man and impious thou art:
Sweet lady, let her pray, and sleep, and dream
Alone with her good angels, far apart
From wicked men like thee. Go, go! – I deem
Thou canst not surely be the same that thou didst seem.'

'I will not harm her, by all saints I swear,'
Quoth Porphyro: 'O may I ne'er find grace
When my weak voice shall whisper its last prayer,
If one of her soft ringlets I displace,
Or look with ruffian passion in her face:
Good Angela, believe me by these tears;
Or I will, even in a moment's space,
Awake, with horrid shout, my foemen's ears,
And beard them, though they be more fanged than wolves and
bears.'

'Ah! why wilt thou affright a feeble soul?
A poor, weak, palsy-stricken, churchyard thing,
Whose passing-bell may ere the midnight toll;
Whose prayers for thee, each morn and evening,
Were never missed.' Thus plaining, doth she bring
A gentler speech from burning Porphyro;
So woeful, and of such deep sorrowing,
That Angela gives promise she will do
Whatever he shall wish, betide her weal or woe.

Which was, to lead him, in close secrecy,
Even to Madeline's chamber, and there hide
Him in a closet, of such privacy
That he might see her beauty unespied,
And win perhaps that night a peerless bride,
While legioned fairies paced the coverlet,
And pale enchantment held her sleepy-eyed.
Never on such a night have lovers met,
Since Merlin paid his Demon all the monstrous debt.

'It shall be as thou wishest,' said the dame:
'All cates and dainties shall be stored there
Quickly on this feast-night: by the tambour frame
Her own lute thou wilt see: no time to spare,
For I am slow and feeble, and scarce dare
On such a catering trust my dizzy head.
Wait here, my child, with patience; kneel in prayer
The while. Ah! thou must needs the lady wed,
Or may I never leave my grave among the dead.'

So saying she hobbled off with busy fear.
The lover's endless minutes slowly passed;
The dame returned, and whispered in his ear
To follow her; with aged eyes aghast
From fright of dim espial. Safe at last,
Through many a dusky gallery, they gain
The maiden's chamber, silken, hushed, and chaste;
Where Porphyro took covert, pleased amain.
His poor guide hurried back with agues in her brain.

Her faltering hand upon the balustrade,
Old Angela was feeling for the stair,
When Madeline, St. Agnes' charmed maid,
Rose, like a missioned spirit, unaware:
With silver taper's light, and pious care,
She turned, and down the aged gossip led
To a safe level matting. Now prepare,
Young Porphyro, for gazing on that bed;
She comes, she comes again, like ring-dove frayed and fled.

Out went the taper as she hurried in;
Its little smoke, in pallid moonshine, died:
She closed the door, she panted, all akin
To spirits of the air, and visions wide:
No uttered syllable, or, woe betide!
But to her heart, her heart was voluble,
Paining with eloquence her balmy side;
As though a tongueless nightingale should swell
Her throat in vain, and die, heart-stifled, in her dell.

A casement high and triple-arched there was,
All garlanded with carven imageries
Of fruits, and flowers, and bunches of knot-grass,
And diamonded with panes of quaint device,
Innumerable of stains and splendid dyes,
As are the tiger-moth's deep-damasked wings;
And in the midst, 'mong thousand heraldries,
And twilight saints, and dim emblazonings,
A shielded scutcheon blushed with blood of queens and kings.

Full on this casement shone the wintry moon,
And threw warm gules on Madeline's fair breast,
As down she knelt for heaven's grace and boon;
Rose-bloom fell on her hands, together pressed,
And on her silver cross soft amethyst,
And on her hair a glory, like a saint:
She seemed a splendid angel, newly dressed,
Save wings, for heaven. Porphyro grew faint:
She knelt, so pure a thing, so free from mortal taint.

Anon his heart revives: her vespers done,
Of all its wreathed pearls her hair she frees;
Unclasps her warmed jewels one by one;
Loosens her fragrant bodice, by degrees
Her rich attire creeps rustling to her knees:
Half-hidden, like a mermaid in seaweed,
Pensive awhile she dreams awake, and sees,
In fancy, fair St. Agnes in her bed,
But dares not look behind, or all the charm is fled.

Soon, trembling in her soft and chilly nest,
In sort of wakeful swoon, perplexed she lay,
Until the poppied warmth of sleep oppressed
Her soothed limbs, and soul fatigued away;
Flown, like a thought, until the morrow-day;
Blissfully havened both from joy and pain;
Clasped like a missal where swart Paynims pray;
Blinded alike from sunshine and from rain,
As though a rose should shut, and be a bud again.

Stolen to this paradise, and so entranced,
Porphyro gazed upon her empty dress,
And listened to her breathing, if it chanced
To wake into a slumberous tenderness;
Which when he heard, that minute did he bless,
And breathed himself: then from the closet crept,
Noiseless as fear in a wide wilderness,
And over the hushed carpet, silent, stepped
And 'tween the curtains peeped, where, lo! – how fast she slept.

Then by the bedside, where the faded moon
Made a dim, silver twilight, soft he set
A table, and, half anguished, threw thereon
A cloth of woven crimson, gold, and jet –
O for some drowsy Morphean amulet!
The boisterous, midnight, festive clarion,
The kettle-drum, and far-heard clarionet,
Affray his ears, though but in dying tone:
The hall door shuts again, and all the noise is gone.

And still she slept an azure-lidded sleep,
In blanched linen, smooth, and lavendered,
While he from forth the closet brought a heap
Of candied apple, quince, and plum, and gourd;
With jellies soother than the creamy curd,
And lucent syrups, tinct with cinnamon;
Manna and dates, in argosy transferred
From Fez; and spiced dainties, every one,
From silken Samarcand to cedared Lebanon.

These delicates he heaped with glowing hand
On golden dishes and in baskets bright
Of wreathed silver: sumptuous they stand
In the retired quiet of the night,
Filling the chilly room with perfume light –
'And now, my love, my seraph fair, awake!
Thou art my heaven, and I thine eremite:
Open thine eyes, for meek St. Agnes' sake,
Or I shall drowse beside thee, so my soul doth ache.'

Thus whispering, his warm, unnerved arm
Sank in her pillow. Shaded was her dream
By the dusk curtains – 'twas a midnight charm
Impossible to melt as iced stream:
The lustrous salvers in the moonlight gleam;
Broad golden fringe upon the carpet lies:
It seemed he never, never could redeem
From such a steadfast spell his lady's eyes;
So mused awhile, entoiled in woofèd phantasies.

Awakening up, he took her hollow lute –
Tumultuous – and, in chords that tenderest be,
He played an ancient ditty, long since mute,
In Provence called, 'La belle dame sans mercy,'
Close to her ear touching the melody;
Wherewith disturbed, she uttered a soft moan:
He ceased – she panted quick – and suddenly
Her blue affrayed eyes wide open shone:
Upon his knees he sank, pale as smooth-sculptured stone.

Her eyes were open, but she still beheld,
Now wide awake, the vision of her sleep:
There was a painful change, that nigh expelled
The blisses of her dream so pure and deep;
At which fair Madeline began to weep,
And moan forth witless words with many a sigh;
While still her gaze on Porphyro would keep;
Who knelt, with joined hands and piteous eye,
Fearing to move or speak, she looked so dreamingly.

'Ah, Porphyro!' said she, 'but even now
Thy voice was at sweet tremble in mine ear,
Made tuneable with every sweetest vow;
And those sad eyes were spiritual and clear:
How changed thou art! how pallid, chill, and drear!
Give me that voice again, my Porphyro,
Those looks immortal, those complainings dear!
Oh leave me not in this eternal woe,
For if thou diest, my love, I know not where to go.'

Beyond a mortal man impassioned far
At these voluptuous accents, he arose,
Ethereal, flushed, and like a throbbing star
Seen mid the sapphire heaven's deep repose;
Into her dream he melted, as the rose
Blendeth its odour with the violet –
Solution sweet: meantime the frost-wind blows
Like love's alarum pattering the sharp sleet
Against the window-panes; St. Agnes' moon hath set.

'Tis dark: quick pattereth the flaw-blown sleet:
'This is no dream, my bride, my Madeline!'
'Tis dark: the iced gusts still rave and beat:
'No dream, alas! alas! and woe is mine!
Porphyro will leave me here to fade and pine –
Cruel! what traitor could thee hither bring?
I curse not, for my heart is lost in thine,
Though thou forsakest a deceived thing –
A dove forlorn and lost with sick unpruned wing.'

'My Madeline! sweet dreamer! lovely bride!
Say, may I be for aye thy vassal blest?
Thy beauty's shield, heart-shaped and vermeil dyed?
Ah, silver shrine, here will I take my rest
After so many hours of toil and quest,
A famished pilgrim, saved by miracle.
Though I have found, I will not rob thy nest
Saving of thy sweet self; if thou think'st well
To trust, fair Madeline, to no rude infidel.

'Hark! 'tis an elfin-storm from faery land,
Of haggard seeming but a boon indeed:
Arise – arise! the morning is at hand;
The bloated wassaillers will never heed:
Let us away, my love, with happy speed;
There are no ears to hear, or eyes to see –
Drowned all in Rhenish and the sleepy mead:
Awake! arise! my love, and fearless be,
For o'er the southern moors I have a home for thee.'

She hurried at his words, beset with fears,
For there were sleeping dragons all around –
At glaring watch, perhaps, with ready spears:
Down the wide stairs a darkling way they found:
In all the house was heard no human sound.
A chain-drooped lamp was flickering by each door;
The arras, rich with horseman, hawk, and hound,
Fluttered in the besieging wind's uproar;
And the long carpets rose along the gusty floor.

They glide, like phantoms, into the wide hall;
Like phantoms, to the iron porch, they glide;
Where lay the porter, in uneasy sprawl,
With a huge empty flagon by his side:
The wakeful bloodhound rose, and shook his hide,
By his sagacious eyes an inmate owns:
By one, and one, the bolts full easy slide:
The chains lie silent on the footworn stones;
The key turns, and the door upon its hinges groans.

And they are gone: ay, ages long ago
These lovers fled away into the storm.
That night the Baron dreamt of many a woe,
And all his warrior-guests, with shade and form
Of witch, and demon, and large coffin-worm,
Were long be-nightmared. Angela the old
Died palsy-twitched, with meagre face deform;
The Beadsman, after thousand aves told,
For aye unsought for slept among his ashes cold.

The Lady of Shalott

Alfred, Lord Tennyson

First published in *Poems* (1833)

PART I

On either side the river lie
Long fields of barley and of rye,
That clothe the wold and meet the sky;
And thro' the field the road runs by
        To many-towered Camelot;
And up and down the people go,
Gazing where the lilies blow
Round an island there below,
        The island of Shalott.

Willows whiten, aspens quiver,
Little breezes dusk and shiver
Thro' the wave that runs for ever
By the island in the river
        Flowing down to Camelot.
Four grey walls, and four grey towers,
Overlook a space of flowers,
And the silent isle embowers
        The Lady of Shalott.

By the margin, willow-veiled,
Slide the heavy barges trailed
By slow horses; and unhailed
The shallop flitteth silken-sailed
        Skimming down to Camelot:
But who hath seen her wave her hand?
Or at the casement seen her stand?
Or is she known in all the land,
        The Lady of Shalott?

Only reapers, reaping early
In among the bearded barley,
Hear a song that echoes cheerly
From the river winding clearly,
        Down to towered Camelot:
And by the moon the reaper weary,
Piling sheaves in uplands airy,
Listening, whispers ''Tis the fairy
        Lady of Shalott.'

PART II

There she weaves by night and day
A magic web with colours gay.
She has heard a whisper say,
A curse is on her if she stay
        To look down to Camelot.
She knows not what the curse may be,
And so she weaveth steadily,
And little other care hath she,
        The Lady of Shalott.

And moving thro' a mirror clear
That hangs before her all the year,
Shadows of the world appear.
There she sees the highway near
        Winding down to Camelot:
There the river eddy whirls,
And there the surly village churls,
And the red cloaks of market girls,
        Pass onward from Shalott.

Sometimes a troop of damsels glad,
An abbot on an ambling pad,
Sometimes a curly shepherd lad,
Or long-haired page in crimson clad,
        Goes by to towered Camelot;
And sometimes thro' the mirror blue
The knights come riding two and two:
She hath no loyal knight and true,
        The Lady of Shalott.

But in her web she still delights
To weave the mirror's magic sights,
For often thro' the silent nights
A funeral, with plumes and lights,
        And music, went to Camelot:
Or when the moon was overhead,
Came two young lovers lately wed;
'I am half sick of shadows,' said
        The Lady of Shalott.

PART III

A bow-shot from her bower-eaves,
He rode between the barley sheaves,
The sun came dazzling thro' the leaves,
And flamed upon the brazen greaves
        Of bold Sir Lancelot.
A red-cross knight for ever kneeled
To a lady in his shield,
That sparkled on the yellow field,
        Beside remote Shalott.

The gemmy bridle glittered free,
Like to some branch of stars we see
Hung in the golden Galaxy.
The bridle bells rang merrily
        As he rode down to Camelot:
And from his blazoned baldric slung
A mighty silver bugle hung,
And as he rode his armour rung,
        Beside remote Shalott.

All in the blue unclouded weather
Thick-jewelled shone the saddle-leather,
The helmet and the helmet-feather
Burned like one burning flame together,
        As he rode down to Camelot.
As often thro' the purple night,
Below the starry clusters bright,
Some bearded meteor, trailing light,
        Moves over still Shalott.

His broad clear brow in sunlight glowed;
On burnished hooves his war-horse trode;
From underneath his helmet flowed
His coal-black curls as on he rode,
As he rode down to Camelot.
From the bank and from the river
He flashed into the crystal mirror,
'Tirra lirra,' by the river
Sang Sir Lancelot.

She left the web, she left the loom,
She made three paces thro' the room,
She saw the water-lily bloom,
She saw the helmet and the plume,
She looked down to Camelot.
Out flew the web and floated wide;
The mirror cracked from side to side;
'The curse is come upon me,' cried
The Lady of Shalott.

PART IV

In the stormy east wind straining,
The pale yellow woods were waning,
The broad stream in his banks complaining,
Heavily the low sky raining
Over towered Camelot;
Down she came and found a boat
Beneath a willow left afloat,
And round about the prow she wrote
The Lady of Shalott.

And down the river's dim expanse –
Like some bold seer in a trance,
Seeing all his own mischance –
With a glassy countenance
        Did she look to Camelot.
And at the closing of the day
She loosed the chain, and down she lay;
The broad stream bore her far away,
        The Lady of Shalott.

Lying, robed in snowy white
That loosely flew to left and right –
The leaves upon her falling light –
Thro' the noises of the night
        She floated down to Camelot:
And as the boat-head wound along
The willowy hills and fields among,
They heard her singing her last song,
        The Lady of Shalott.

Heard a carol, mournful, holy,
Chanted loudly, chanted lowly,
Till her blood was frozen slowly,
And her eyes were darkened wholly,
        Turned to towered Camelot;
For ere she reached upon the tide
The first house by the waterside,
Singing in her song she died,
        The Lady of Shalott.

Under tower and balcony,
By garden wall and gallery,
A gleaming shape she floated by,
Dead-pale between the houses high,
Silent into Camelot.
Out upon the wharfs they came,
Knight and burgher, lord and dame,
And round the prow they read her name,
The Lady of Shalott.

Who is this? and what is here?
And in the lighted palace near
Died the sound of royal cheer;
And they crossed themselves for fear,
All the knights at Camelot:
But Lancelot mused a little space;
He said, 'She has a lovely face;
God in his mercy lend her grace,
The Lady of Shalott.'

The Jackdaw of Rheims

Richard Harris Barham

First published under the pseudonym of Thomas Ingoldsby in *Bentley's Monthly Miscellany*, May 1837

THE jackdaw sat on the Cardinal's chair!
Bishop, and abbott, and prior were there;
  Many a monk, and many a friar,
  Many a knight, and many a squire,
With a great many more of lesser degree –
In sooth a goodly company;
And they served the Lord Primate on bended knee.
  Never, I ween,
  Was a prouder seen,
Read of in books, or dreamt of in dreams,
Than the Cardinal Lord Archbishop of Rheims!

  In and out
  Through the motley rout,
That little jackdaw kept hopping about;
  Here and there
  Like a dog in a fair,
  Over comfits and cates,
  And dishes and plates,
Cowl and cope, and rochet and pall,
Mitre and crosier! he hopped upon all!
  With saucy air,
  He perched on the chair

Where, in state, the great Lord Cardinal sat
In the great Lord Cardinal's great red hat;
  And he peered in the face
  Of his Lordship's Grace,
With a satisfied look, as if he would say,
'We two are the greatest folks here today!'
  And the priests with awe,
  As such freaks they saw,
Said, 'The Devil must be in that little jackdaw!'

The feast was over, the board was cleared,
The flawns and the custards had all disappeared,
And six little singing-boys – dear little souls!
In nice clean faces, and nice white stoles,
  Came, in order due,
  Two by two,
Marching that grand refectory through.
A nice little boy held a golden ewer,
Embossed and filled with water, as pure
As any that flows between Rheims and Namur,
Which a nice little boy stood ready to catch
In a fine golden hand-basin made to match.
Two nice little boys, rather more grown,
Carried lavender water, and Eau de Cologne;
And a nice little boy had a nice cake of soap,
Worthy of washing the hands of the Pope.
  One little boy more
  A napkin bore,
Of the best white diaper, fringed with pink,
And a Cardinal's Hat marked in permanent ink.

The great Lord Cardinal turns at the sight
Of these nice little boys dressed all in white:
  From his finger he draws
  His costly turquoise;
And, not thinking at all about little jackdaws,
  Deposits it straight
  By the side of his plate,
While the nice little boys on his Eminence wait;
Till, when nobody's dreaming of any such thing,
That little jackdaw hops off with the ring!

  There's a cry and a shout,
  And a deuce of a rout,
And nobody seems to know what they're about,
But the monks have their pockets all turned inside out.
  The friars are kneeling,
  And hunting and feeling
The carpet, the floor, and the walls, and the ceiling.
  The Cardinal drew
  Off each plum-coloured shoe,
And left his red stockings exposed to the view;
  He peeps and he feels
  In the toes and the heels;
They turn up the dishes, they turn up the plates,
They take up the poker and poke out the grates,
  – They turn up the rugs,
  They examine the mugs:
  But, no! – no such thing –
  They can't find THE RING!
And the Abbot declared that 'when nobody twigged it,
Some rascal or other had popped in and prigged it'.

The Cardinal rose with a dignified look,
He called for his candle, his bell, and his book.
  In holy anger and pious grief,
  He solemnly cursed that rascally thief.
  He cursed him at board, he cursed him in bed;
  From the sole of his foot to the crown of his head;
  He cursed him in sleeping, that every night
  He should dream of the devil, and wake in a fright;
  He cursed him in eating, he cursed him in drinking,
  He cursed him in coughing, in sneezing, in winking;
  He cursed him in sitting, in standing, in lying;
  He cursed him in walking, in riding, in flying;
  He cursed him in living, he cursed him in dying.
Never was heard such a terrible curse!
  But what gave rise
  To no little surprise,
Nobody seemed one penny the worse!

  The day was gone,
  The night came on,
The monks and the friars they searched till dawn;
  When the Sacristan saw,
  On crumpled claw,
Come limping a poor little lame jackdaw!
  No longer gay,
  As on yesterday;
His feathers all seemed to be turned the wrong way;
His pinions drooped, he could hardly stand,
His head was as bald as the palm of your hand;
  His eye so dim,
  So wasted each limb,

That, heedless of grammar, they all cried, 'THAT'S HIM! –
That's the scamp that has done this scandalous thing!
That's the thief that has got my Lord Cardinal's ring!'

  The poor little jackdaw,
  When the monks he saw,
Feebly gave vent to the ghost of a caw;
And turned his bald head, as much as to say,
'Pray, be so good as to walk this way!'
  Slower and slower
  He limped on before,
Till they came to the back of the belfry door,
  Where the first thing they saw,
  Midst the sticks and the straw,
Was the RING in the nest of that little jackdaw!

Then the great Lord Cardinal called for his book,
And off that terrible curse he took;
  The mute expression
  Served in lieu of confession,
And, being thus coupled with full restitution,
The jackdaw got plenary absolution.
  – When those words were heard,
  That poor little bird
Was so changed in a moment, 'twas really absurd.
  He grew sleek and fat;
  In addition to that,
A fresh crop of feathers came thick as a mat.
  His tail waggled more
  Even than before;
But no longer it wagged with an impudent air,
No longer he perched on the Cardinal's chair.

He hopped now about
With a gait devout;
At Matins, at Vespers, he never was out;
And, so far from any more pilfering deeds,
He always seemed telling the Confessor's beads.
If anyone lied, or if anyone swore,
Or slumbered in prayer-time and happened to snore,
That good jackdaw
Would give a great 'Caw!'
As much as to say, 'Don't do so any more!'
While many remarked, as his manners they saw,
That they 'never had known such a pious jackdaw!'
He long lived the pride
Of that countryside,
And at last in the odour of sanctity died;

When, as words were too faint
His merits to paint,
The Conclave determined to make him a Saint;
And on newly-made Saints and Popes, as you know,
It's the custom at Rome, new names to bestow,
So they canonized him by the name of Jim Crow!

Horatius (abridged)

Thomas Babington Macaulay, Lord Macaulay

First published in *Lays of Ancient Rome* (1842)

Lars Porsena of Clusium
  By the Nine Gods he swore
That the great house of Tarquin
  Should suffer wrong no more.
By the Nine Gods he swore it,
  And named a trysting day,
And bade his messengers ride forth,
East and west and south and north,
  To summon his array.

East and west and south and north
  The messengers ride fast,
And tower and town and cottage
  Have heard the trumpet's blast.
Shame on the false Etruscan
  Who lingers in his home,
When Porsena of Clusium
  Is on the march for Rome.

The horsemen and the footmen
  Are pouring in amain
From many a stately market-place;
  From many a fruitful plain;

From many a lonely hamlet,
   Which, hid by beech and pine,
Like an eagle's nest, hangs on the crest
   Of purple Apennine.

And now hath every city
   Sent up her tale of men;
The foot are fourscore thousand,
   The horse are thousands ten.
Before the gates of Sutrium
   Is met the great array.
A proud man was Lars Porsena
   Upon the trysting day.

But by the yellow Tiber
   Was tumult and affright:
From all the spacious champaign
   To Rome men took their flight.
A mile around the city,
   The throng stopped up the ways;
A fearful sight it was to see
   Through two long nights and days.

Now, from the rock Tarpeian,
   Could the wan burghers spy
The line of blazing villages
   Red in the midnight sky.
The Fathers of the City,
   They sat all night and day,
For every hour some horseman came
   With tidings of dismay.

I wis, in all the Senate,
  There was no heart so bold,
But sore it ached, and fast it beat,
  When that ill news was told.
Forthwith up rose the Consul,
  Up rose the Fathers all;
In haste they girded up their gowns,
  And hied them to the wall.

They held a council standing
  Before the River Gate;
Short time was there, ye well may guess,
  For musing or debate.
Out spake the Consul roundly:
  'The bridge must straight go down;
For, since Janiculum is lost,
  Nought else can save the town.'

Just then a scout came flying,
  All wild with haste and fear:
'To arms! to arms! Sir Consul:
  Lars Porsena is here.'
On the low hills to westward
  The Consul fixed his eye,
And saw the swarthy storm of dust
  Rise fast along the sky.

And nearer fast and nearer
  Doth the red whirlwind come;
And louder still and still more loud,
From underneath that rolling cloud,
Is heard the trumpet's war-note proud,
  The trampling, and the hum.

And plainly and more plainly
  Now through the gloom appears,
Far to left and far to right,
In broken gleams of dark-blue light,
The long array of helmets bright,
  The long array of spears.

But the Consul's brow was sad,
  And the Consul's speech was low,
And darkly looked he at the wall,
  And darkly at the foe.
'Their van will be upon us
  Before the bridge goes down;
And if they once may win the bridge,
  What hope to save the town?'

Then out spake brave Horatius,
  The Captain of the Gate:
'To every man upon this earth
  Death cometh soon or late.
And how can man die better
  Than facing fearful odds,
For the ashes of his fathers,
  And the temples of his Gods?

'Hew down the bridge, Sir Consul,
  With all the speed ye may;
I, with two more to help me,
  Will hold the foe in play.
In yon straight path a thousand
  May well be stopped by three.
Now who will stand on either hand,
  And keep the bridge with me?'

Then out spake Spurius Lartius;
  A Ramnian proud was he:
'Lo, I will stand at thy right hand,
  And keep the bridge with thee.'
And out spake strong Herminius;
  Of Titian blood was he:
'I will abide on thy left side,
  And keep the bridge with thee.'

'Horatius,' quoth the Consul,
  'As thou sayest, so let it be.'
And straight against that great array
  Forth went the dauntless Three.
For Romans in Rome's quarrel
  Spared neither land nor gold,
Nor son nor wife, nor limb nor life,
  In the brave days of old.

Then none was for a party;
  Then all were for the state;
Then the great man helped the poor,
  And the poor man loved the great:
Then lands were fairly portioned;
  Then spoils were fairly sold:
The Romans were like brothers
  In the brave days of old.

Now while the Three were tightening
  Their harness on their backs,
The Consul was the foremost man
  To take in hand an axe:
And Fathers mixed with Commons
  Seized hatchet, bar, and crow,

And smote upon the planks above,
  And loosed the props below.

Meanwhile the Tuscan army,
  Right glorious to behold,
Came, flashing back the noonday light,
Rank behind rank, like surges bright
  Of a broad sea of gold.
Four hundred trumpets sounded
  A peal of warlike glee,
As that great host, with measured tread,
And spears advanced, and ensigns spread,
Rolled slowly towards the bridge's head,
  Where stood the dauntless Three.

The Three stood calm and silent,
  And looked upon the foes,
And a great shout of laughter
  From all the vanguard rose:
And forth three chiefs came spurring
  Before that deep array;
To earth they sprang, their swords they drew,
And lifted high their shields, and flew
  To win the narrow way;

Aunus from green Tifernum,
  Lord of the Hill of Vines;
And Seius, whose eight hundred slaves
  Sicken in Ilva's mines;
And Picus, long to Clusium
  Vassal in peace and war,
Who led to fight his Umbrian powers
From that grey crag where, girt with towers,

The fortress of Nequinum lowers
  O'er the pale waves of Nar.

Stout Lartius hurled down Aunus
  Into the stream beneath:
Herminius struck at Seius,
  And clove him to the teeth:
At Picus brave Horatius
  Darted one fiery thrust;
And the proud Umbrian's gilded arms
  Clashed in the bloody dust.

Then Ocnus of Falerii
  Rushed on the Roman Three;
And Lausulus of Urgo,
  The rover of the sea;
And Aruns of Volsinium,
  Who slew the great wild boar,
The great wild boar that had his den
Amidst the reeds of Cosa's fen,
And wasted fields, and slaughtered men,
  Along Albinia's shore.

Herminius smote down Aruns:
  Lartius laid Ocnus low:
Right to the heart of Lausulus
  Horatius sent a blow.
'Lie there,' he cried, 'fell pirate!
  No more, aghast and pale,
From Ostia's walls the crowd shall mark
The track of thy destroying bark.

No more Campania's hinds shall fly
To woods and caverns when they spy
  Thy thrice accursed sail.'

But now no sound of laughter
  Was heard among the foes.
A wild and wrathful clamour
  From all the vanguard rose.
Six spears' lengths from the entrance
  Halted that deep array,
And for a space no man came forth
  To win the narrow way.

But hark! the cry is Astur:
  And lo! the ranks divide;
And the great Lord of Luna
  Comes with his stately stride.
Upon his ample shoulders
  Clangs loud the four-fold shield,
And in his hand he shakes the brand
  Which none but he can wield.

He smiled on those bold Romans
  A smile serene and high;
He eyed the flinching Tuscans,
  And scorn was in his eye.
Quoth he, 'The she-wolf's litter
  Stand savagely at bay:
But will ye dare to follow,
  If Astur clears the way?'

Then, whirling up his broadsword
  With both hands to the height,

He rushed against Horatius,
   And smote with all his might.
With shield and blade Horatius
   Right deftly turned the blow.
The blow, though turned, came yet too nigh;
It missed his helm, but gashed his thigh:
The Tuscans raised a joyful cry
   To see the red blood flow.

He reeled, and on Herminius
   He leaned one breathing-space;
Then, like a wild cat mad with wounds,
   Sprang right at Astur's face.
Through teeth, and skull, and helmet
   So fierce a thrust he sped,
The good sword stood a hand-breadth out
   Behind the Tuscan's head.

And the great Lord of Luna
   Fell at that deadly stroke,
As falls on Mount Alvernus
   A thunder-smitten oak.
Far o'er the crashing forest
   The giant arms lie spread;
And the pale augurs, muttering low,
   Gaze on the blasted head.

On Astur's throat Horatius
   Right firmly pressed his heel,
And thrice and four times tugged amain,
   Ere he wrenched out the steel.
'And see,' he cried, 'the welcome,

Fair guests, that waits you here!
What noble Lucumo comes next
To taste our Roman cheer?'

But at his haughty challenge
A sullen murmur ran,
Mingled of wrath, and shame, and dread,
Along that glittering van.
There lacked not men of prowess,
Nor men of lordly race;
For all Etruria's noblest
Were round the fatal place.

But all Etruria's noblest
Felt their hearts sink to see
On the earth the bloody corpses,
In the path the dauntless Three:
And, from the ghastly entrance
Where those bold Romans stood,
All shrank, like boys who unaware,
Ranging the woods to start a hare,
Come to the mouth of the dark lair
Where, growling low, a fierce old bear
Lies amidst bones and blood.

Was none who would be foremost
To lead such dire attack:
But those behind cried 'Forward!'
And those before cried 'Back!'
And backward now and forward
Wavers the deep array;
And on the tossing sea of steel,
To and fro the standards reel;

And the victorious trumpet-peal
  Dies fitfully away.

But meanwhile axe and lever
  Have manfully been plied;
And now the bridge hangs tottering
  Above the boiling tide.
'Come back, come back, Horatius!'
  Loud cried the Fathers all.
'Back, Lartius! back, Herminius!
  Back, ere the ruin fall!'

Back darted Spurius Lartius;
  Herminius darted back:
And, as they passed, beneath their feet
  They felt the timbers crack.
But when they turned their faces,
  And on the farther shore
Saw brave Horatius stand alone,
  They would have crossed once more.

But with a crash like thunder
  Fell every loosened beam,
And, like a dam, the mighty wreck
  Lay right athwart the stream:
And a long shout of triumph
  Rose from the walls of Rome,
As to the highest turret-tops
  Was splashed the yellow foam.

And, like a horse unbroken
  When first he feels the rein,
The furious river struggled hard,

And tossed his tawny mane,
And burst the curb, and bounded,
Rejoicing to be free,
And whirling down, in fierce career,
Battlement, and plank, and pier,
Rushed headlong to the sea.

Alone stood brave Horatius,
But constant still in mind;
Thrice thirty thousand foes before,
And the broad flood behind.
'Down with him!' cried false Sextus,
With a smile on his pale face.
'Now yield thee,' cried Lars Porsena,
'Now yield thee to our grace.'

Round turned he, as not deigning
Those craven ranks to see;
Nought spake he to Lars Porsena,
To Sextus nought spake he;
But he saw on Palatinus
The white porch of his home;
And he spake to the noble river
That rolls by the towers of Rome.

'Oh, Tiber! father Tiber!
To whom the Romans pray,
A Roman's life, a Roman's arms,
Take thou in charge this day!'
So he spake, and speaking sheathed
The good sword by his side,
And with his harness on his back,
Plunged headlong in the tide.

No sound of joy or sorrow
  Was heard from either bank;
But friends and foes in dumb surprise,
With parted lips and straining eyes,
  Stood gazing where he sank;
And when above the surges
  They saw his crest appear,
All Rome sent forth a rapturous cry,
And even the ranks of Tuscany
  Could scarce forbear to cheer.

But fiercely ran the current,
  Swollen high by months of rain:
And fast his blood was flowing;
  And he was sore in pain,
And heavy with his armour,
  And spent with changing blows:
And oft they thought him sinking,
  But still again he rose.

Never, I ween, did swimmer,
  In such an evil case,
Struggle through such a raging flood
  Safe to the landing-place:
But his limbs were borne up bravely
  By the brave heart within
And our good father Tiber
  Bare bravely up his chin.

And now he feels the bottom;
  Now on dry earth he stands;
Now round him throng the Fathers
  To press his gory hands;

And now, with shouts and clapping,
And noise of weeping loud,
He enters through the River Gate,
Borne by the joyous crowd.

They gave him of the corn-land,
That was of public right,
As much as two strong oxen
Could plough from morn till night;
And they made a molten image,
And set it up on high,
And there it stands unto this day
To witness if I lie.

It stands in the Comitium,
Plain for all folk to see;
Horatius in his harness,
Halting upon one knee:
And underneath is written,
In letters all of gold,
How valiantly he kept the bridge
In the brave days of old.

The Pied Piper of Hamelin

Robert Browning

First published in *Dramatic Lyrics* (1842)

Hamelin Town's in Brunswick,
  By famous Hanover city;
The river Weser, deep and wide,
Washes its wall on the southern side;
A pleasanter spot you never spied;
  But, when begins my ditty,
Almost five hundred years ago,
To see the townsfolk suffer so
  From vermin, was a pity.

  Rats!
They fought the dogs and killed the cats,
  And bit the babies in the cradles,
And ate the cheeses out of the vats,
  And licked the soup from the cooks' own ladles,
Split open the kegs of salted sprats,
Made nests inside men's Sunday hats,
And even spoiled the women's chats
    By drowning their speaking
    With shrieking and squeaking
In fifty different sharps and flats.

At last the people in a body
   To the Town Hall came flocking:
''Tis clear,' cried they, 'our Mayor's a noddy;

And as for our Corporation – shocking
To think we buy gowns lined with ermine
For dolts that can't or won't determine
What's best to rid us of our vermin!
You hope, because you're old and obese,
To find in the furry civic robe ease?
Rouse up, sirs! Give your brains a racking
To find the remedy we're lacking,
Or, sure as fate, we'll send you packing!'
At this the Mayor and Corporation
Quaked with a mighty consternation.

An hour they sat in council,
At length the Mayor broke silence:
'For a guilder I'd my ermine gown sell,
I wish I were a mile hence!
It's easy to bid one rack one's brain –
I'm sure my poor head aches again,
I've scratched it so, and all in vain.
Oh for a trap, a trap, a trap!'
Just as he said this, what should hap
At the chamber door but a gentle tap?
'Bless us,' cried the Mayor, 'what's that?'
(With the Corporation as he sat,
Looking little though wondrous fat;
Nor brighter was his eye, nor moister
Than a too-long-opened oyster,
Save when at noon his paunch grew mutinous
For a plate of turtle, green and glutinous),
'Only a scraping of shoes on the mat?
Anything like the sound of a rat
Makes my heart go pit-a-pat!'

'Come in!' the Mayor cried, looking bigger:
And in did come the strangest figure!
His queer long coat from heel to head
Was half of yellow and half of red,
And he himself was tall and thin,
With sharp blue eyes, each like a pin,
And light loose hair, yet swarthy skin,
No tuft on cheek nor beard on chin,
But lips where smiles went out and in;
There was no guessing his kith and kin:
And nobody could enough admire
The tall man and his quaint attire.
Quoth one: 'It's as my great-grandsire,
Starting up at the Trump of Doom's tone,
Had walked this way from his painted tombstone!'

He advanced to the council-table:
And, 'Please your honours,' said he, 'I'm able,
By means of a secret charm, to draw
  All creatures living beneath the sun,
  That creep or swim or fly or run,
After me so as you never saw!
And I chiefly use my charm
On creatures that do people harm,
The mole and toad and newt and viper;
And people call me the Pied Piper.'
(And here they noticed round his neck
  A scarf of red and yellow stripe,
To match with his coat of the self-same check;
  And at the scarf's end hung a pipe;
And his fingers, they noticed, were ever straying
As if impatient to be playing

Upon this pipe, as low it dangled
Over his vesture so old-fangled.)
'Yet,' said he, 'poor piper as I am,
In Tartary I freed the Cham,
    Last June, from his huge swarms of gnats;
I eased in Asia the Nizam
    Of a monstrous brood of vampire-bats:
And as for what your brain bewilders,
    If I can rid your town of rats
Will you give me a thousand guilders?'
'One? fifty thousand!' – was the exclamation
Of the astonished Mayor and Corporation.

Into the street the Piper stept,
    Smiling first a little smile,
As if he knew what magic slept
    In his quiet pipe the while;
Then, like a musical adept,
To blow the pipe his lips he wrinkled,
And green and blue his sharp eyes twinkled,
Like a candle-flame where salt is sprinkled;
And ere three shrill notes the pipe uttered,
You heard as if an army muttered;
And the muttering grew to a grumbling;
And the grumbling grew to a mighty rumbling;
And out of the houses the rats came tumbling.
Great rats, small rats, lean rats, brawny rats,
Brown rats, black rats, grey rats, tawny rats,
Grave old plodders, gay young friskers,
    Father, mothers, uncles, cousins,
Cocking tails and pricking whiskers,
    Families by tens and dozens,
Brothers, sisters, husbands, wives –

Followed the Piper for their lives.
From street to street he piped advancing,
And step for step they followed dancing,
Until they came to the river Weser,
  Wherein all plunged and perished!
– Save one who, stout as Julius Caesar,
Swam across and lived to carry
  (As he, the manuscript he cherished)
To Rat-land home his commentary:
Which was, 'At the first shrill notes of the pipe,
I heard a sound as of scraping tripe,
And putting apples, wondrous ripe,
Into a cider-press's gripe:
And a moving away of pickle-tub-boards,
And a leaving ajar of conserve-cupboards,
And a drawing the corks of train-oil-flasks,
And a breaking the hoops of butter-casks;
And it seemed as if a voice
  (Sweeter far than by harp or by psaltery
Is breathed) called out, "Oh rats, rejoice!
  The world is grown to one vast drysaltery!
So munch on, crunch on, take your nuncheon,
Breakfast, supper, dinner, luncheon!"
And just as the bulky sugar-puncheon,
All ready staved, like a great sun shone
Glorious scarce an inch before me,
Just as methought it said, "Come, bore me!"
– I found the Weser rolling o'er me.'

You should have heard the Hamelin people
Ringing the bells till they rocked the steeple.
'Go,' cried the Mayor, 'and get long poles,
Poke out the nests and block up the holes!

Consult with carpenters and builders,
And leave in our town not even a trace
Of the rats!' – when suddenly, up the face
Of the Piper perked in the market-place,
With a 'First, if you please, my thousand guilders!'

A thousand guilders! The Mayor looked blue;
So did the Corporation too.
For council dinners made rare havoc
With Claret, Moselle, Vin-de-Grave, Hock;
And half the money would replenish
Their cellar's biggest butt with Rhenish.
To pay this sum to a wandering fellow
With a gipsy coat of red and yellow!
'Beside,' quoth the Mayor with a knowing wink,
'Our business was done at the river's brink;
We saw with our eyes the vermin sink,
And what's dead can't come to life, I think.
So, friend, we're not the folks to shrink
From the duty of giving you something for drink,
And a matter of money to put in your poke;
But as for the guilders, what we spoke
Of them, as you very well know, was in joke.
Besides, our losses have made us thrifty.
A thousand guilders! Come, take fifty!'

The Piper's face fell, and he cried,
'No trifling! I can't wait, beside!
I've promised to visit by dinnertime
Baghdad, and accept the prime
Of the Head-Cook's pottage, all he's rich in,
For having left, in the Caliph's kitchen,
Of a nest of scorpions no survivor:

With him I proved no bargain-driver,
With you, don't think I'll bate a stiver!
And folks who put me in a passion
May find me pipe after another fashion.'
'How?' cried the Mayor, 'd'ye think I brook
Being worse treated than a cook?
Insulted by a lazy ribald
With idle pipe and vesture piebald?
You threaten us, fellow? Do your worst,
Blow your pipe there till you burst!'

Once more he stepped into the steet
And to his lips again
Laid his long pipe of smooth straight cane;
And ere he blew three notes (such sweet
Soft notes as yet musician's cunning
Never gave the enraptured air)
There was a rustling that seemed like a bustling
Of merry crowds justling at pitching and hustling,
Small feet were pattering, wooden shoes clattering,
Little hands clapping and little tongues chattering,
And, like fowls in a farmyard when barley is scattering,
Out came the children running.
All the little boys and girls,
With rosy cheeks and flaxen curls,
And sparkling eyes and teeth like pearls,
Tripping and skipping, ran merrily after
The wonderful music with shouting and laughter.

The Mayor was dumb, and the Council stood
As if they were changed into blocks of wood,
Unable to move a step, or cry
To the children merrily skipping by

– Could only follow with the eye
That joyous crowd at the Piper's back.
But how the Mayor was on the rack,
And the wretched Council's bosoms beat,
As the Piper turned from the High Street
To where the Weser rolled its waters
Right in the way of their sons and daughters!
However he turned from south to west,
And to Koppelberg Hill his steps addressed,
And after him the children pressed;
Great was the joy in every breast.
'He never can cross that mighty top!
He's forced to let the piping drop,
And we shall see our children stop!'
When, lo, as they reached the mountain-side,
A wondrous portal opened wide,
As if a cavern was suddenly hollowed;
And the Piper advanced and the children followed,
And when all were in to the very last,
The door in the mountain-side shut fast.
Did I say, all? No! One was lame,
  And could not dance the whole of the way;
And in after years, if you would blame
  His sadness, he was used to say –
'It's dull in our town since my playmates left!
I can't forget that I'm bereft
Of all the pleasant sights they see,
Which the Piper also promised me.
For he led us, he said, to a joyous land,
Joining the town and just at hand,
Where waters gushed and fruit trees grew
And flowers put forth a fairer hue,
And everything was strange and new;

The sparrows were brighter than peacocks here,
And their dogs outran our fallow deer,
And honey-bees had lost their stings,
And horses were born with eagles' wings:
And just as I became assured
My lame foot would be speedily cured,
The music stopped and I stood still,
And found myself outside the hill,
Left alone against my will,
To go now limping as before,
And never hear of that country more!'

Alas, alas for Hamelin!
  There came into many a burgher's pate
  A text which says that heaven's gate
  Opes to the rich at as easy rate
As the needle's eye takes a camel in!
The Mayor sent east, west, north, and south,
To offer the Piper, by word of mouth,
  Wherever it was men's lot to find him,
Silver and gold to his heart's content,
If he'd only return the way he went,
  And bring the children behind him.
But when they saw 'twas a lost endeavour,
And Piper and dancers were gone for ever,
They made a decree that lawyers never
  Should think their records dated duly
If, after the day of the month and year,
These words did not as well appear,
'And so long after what happened here
  On the Twenty-second of July,
Thirteen hundred and seventy-six':
And the better in memory to fix

The place of the children's last retreat,
They called it the Pied Piper's Street –
Where anyone playing on pipe or tabor
Was sure for the future to lose his labour.
Nor suffered they hostelry or tavern
  To shock with mirth a street so solemn;
But opposite the place of the cavern
  They wrote the story on a column;
And on the great church-window painted
The same, to make the world acquainted
How their children were stolen away,
And there it stands to this very day.
And I must not omit to say
That in Transylvania there's a tribe
Of alien people who ascribe
The outlandish ways and dress
On which their neighbours lay such stress,
To their fathers and mothers having risen
Out of some subterraneous prison
Into which they were trepanned
Long time ago in a mighty band
Out of Hamelin town in Brunswick land,
But how or why, they don't understand.

Childe Roland to the Dark Tower Came

Robert Browning

First published in *Men and Women* (1855)

My first thought was, he lied in every word,
  That hoary cripple, with malicious eye
  Askance to watch the working of his lie
On mine, and mouth scarce able to afford
Suppression of the glee, that pursed and scored
  Its edge, at one more victim gained thereby.

What else should he be set for, with his staff?
  What, save to waylay with his lies, ensnare
  All travellers who might find him posted there,
And ask the road? I guessed what skull-like laugh
Would break, what crutch 'gin write my epitaph
  For pastime in the dusty thoroughfare,

If at his counsel I should turn aside
  Into that ominous tract which, all agree,
  Hides the Dark Tower. Yet acquiescingly
I did turn as he pointed: neither pride
Nor hope rekindling at the end descried,
  So much as gladness that some end might be.

For, what with my whole world-wide wandering,
What with my search drawn out through years, my hope
Dwindled into a ghost not fit to cope
With that obstreperous joy success would bring –
I hardly tried now to rebuke the spring
My heart made, finding failure in its scope.

As when a sick man very near to death
Seems dead indeed, and feels begin and end
The tears and takes the farewell of each friend,
And hears one bid the other go, draw breath
Freelier outside ('since all is o'er,' he saith,
'And the blow fallen no grieving can amend');

While some discuss if near the other graves
Be room enough for this, and when a day
Suits best for carrying the corpse away,
With care about the banners, scarves and staves:
And still the man hears all, and only craves
He may not shame such tender love and stay.

Thus, I had so long suffered in this quest,
Heard failure prophesied so oft, been writ
So many times among 'The Band' – to wit,
The knights who to the Dark Tower's search addressed
Their steps – that just to fail as they, seemed best,
And all the doubt was now – should I be fit?

So, quiet as despair, I turned from him,
That hateful cripple, out of his highway
Into the path he pointed. All the day
Had been a dreary one at best, and dim
Was settling to its close, yet shot one grim
Red leer to see the plain catch its estray.

For mark! no sooner was I fairly found
  Pledged to the plain, after a pace or two,
  Than, pausing to throw backward a last view
O'er the safe road, 'twas gone; grey plain all round:
Nothing but plain to the horizon's bound.
  I might go on; nought else remained to do.

So, on I went. I think I never saw
  Such starved ignoble nature; nothing throve:
  For flowers – as well expect a cedar grove!
But cockle, spurge, according to their law
Might propagate their kind, with none to awe,
  You'd think; a burr had been a treasure trove.

No! penury, inertness and grimace,
  In some strange sort, were the land's portion. 'See
  Or shut your eyes,' said Nature peevishly,
'It nothing skills: I cannot help my case:
'Tis the Last Judgment's fire must cure this place,
  Calcine its clods and set my prisoners free.'

If there pushed any ragged thistle stalk
  Above its mates, the head was chopped; the bents
  Were jealous else. What made those holes and rents
In the dock's harsh swarth leaves, bruised as to baulk
All hope of greenness? 'tis a brute must walk
  Pashing their life out, with a brute's intents.

As for the grass, it grew as scant as hair
  In leprosy; thin dry blades pricked the mud
  Which underneath looked kneaded up with blood.
One stiff blind horse, his every bone a-stare,
Stood stupefied, however he came there:
  Thrust out past service from the devil's stud!

Alive? he might be dead for aught I know,
With that red gaunt and colloped neck a-strain,
And shut eyes underneath the rusty mane;
Seldom went such grotesqueness with such woe;
I never saw a brute I hated so;
He must be wicked to deserve such pain.

I shut my eyes and turned them on my heart.
As a man calls for wine before he fights,
I asked one draught of earlier, happier sights,
Ere fitly I could hope to play my part.
Think first, fight afterwards – the soldier's art:
One taste of the old time sets all to rights.

Not it! I fancied Cuthbert's reddening face
Beneath its garniture of curly gold,
Dear fellow, till I almost felt him fold
An arm in mine to fix me to the place,
That way he used. Alas, one night's disgrace!
Out went my heart's new fire and left it cold.

Giles then, the soul of honour – there he stands
Frank as ten years ago when knighted first.
What honest men should dare (he said) he durst.
Good – but the scene shifts – faugh! what hangman-hands
Pin to his breast a parchment? his own bands
Read it. Poor traitor, spit upon and curst!

Better this present than a past like that;
Back therefore to my darkening path again!
No sound, no sight as far as eye could strain.
Will the night send a howlet or a bat?
I asked: when something on the dismal flat
Came to arrest my thoughts and change their train.

A sudden little river crossed my path
  As unexpected as a serpent comes.
  No sluggish tide congenial to the glooms;
This, as it frothed by, might have been a bath
For the fiend's glowing hoof – to see the wrath
  Of its black eddy bespate with flakes and spumes.

So petty yet so spiteful! All along,
  Low scrubby alders kneeled down over it;
  Drenched willows flung them headlong in a fit
Of mute despair, a suicidal throng:
The river which had done them all the wrong,
  Whate'er that was, rolled by, deterred no whit.

Which, while I forded – good saints, how I feared
  To set my foot upon a dead man's cheek,
  Each step, or feel the spear I thrust to seek
For hollows, tangled in his hair or beard!
– It may have been a water-rat I speared,
  But, ugh! it sounded like a baby's shriek.

Glad was I when I reached the other bank.
  Now for a better country. Vain presage!
  Who were the strugglers, what war did they wage,
Whose savage trample thus could pad the dank
Soil to a plash? Toads in a poisoned tank,
  Or wild cats in a red-hot iron cage –

The fight must so have seemed in that fell cirque.
  What penned them there, with all the plain to choose?
  No footprint leading to that horrid mews,
None out of it. Mad brewage set to work
Their brains, no doubt, like galley-slaves the Turk
  Pits for his pastime, Christians against Jews.

And more than that – a furlong on – why, there!
  What bad use was that engine for, that wheel,
  Or brake, not wheel – that harrow fit to reel
Men's bodies out like silk? with all the air
Of Tophet's tool, on earth left unaware,
  Or brought to sharpen its rusty teeth of steel.

Then came a bit of stubbed ground, once a wood,
  Next a marsh, it would seem, and now mere earth
  Desperate and done with (so a fool finds mirth,
Makes a thing and then mars it, till his mood
Changes and off he goes!) within a rood –
  Bog, clay and rubble, sand and stark black dearth.

Now blotches rankling, coloured gay and grim,
  Now patches where some leanness of the soil's
  Broke into moss or substances like boils;
Then came some palsied oak, a cleft in him
Like a distorted mouth that splits its rim
  Gaping at death, and dies while it recoils.

And just as far as ever from the end!
  Nought in the distance but the evening, nought
  To point my footstep further! At the thought,
A great black bird, Apollyon's bosom friend,
Sailed past, nor beat his wide wing dragon-penned
  That brushed my cap – perchance the guide I sought.

For, looking up, aware I somehow grew,
  'Spite of the dusk, the plain had given place
  All round to mountains – with such name to grace
Mere ugly heights and heaps now stolen in view.
How thus they had surprised me – solve it, you!
  How to get from them was no clearer case.

Yet half I seemed to recognize some trick
Of mischief happened to me, God knows when –
In a bad dream perhaps. Here ended, then,
Progress this way. When, in the very nick
Of giving up, one time more, came a click
As when a trap shuts – you're inside the den!

Burningly it came on me all at once,
This was the place! those two hills on the right,
Crouched like two bulls locked horn in horn in fight;
While to the left, a tall scalped mountain . . . Dunce,
Dotard, a-dozing at the very nonce,
After a life spent training for the sight!

What in the midst lay but the Tower itself?
The round squat turret, blind as the fool's heart,
Built of brown stone, without a counterpart
In the whole world. The tempest's mocking elf
Points to the shipman thus the unseen shelf
He strikes on, only when the timbers start.

Not see? because of night perhaps? – why, day
Came back again for that! before it left,
The dying sunset kindled through a cleft:
The hills, like giants at a hunting, lay,
Chin upon hand, to see the game at bay –
'Now stab and end the creature – to the heft!'

Not hear? when noise was everywhere! it tolled
Increasing like a bell. Names in my ears
Of all the lost adventurers my peers –
How such a one was strong, and such was bold,
And such was fortunate, yet each of old
Lost, lost! one moment knelled the woe of years.

There they stood, ranged along the hillsides, met
  To view the last of me, a living frame
  For one more picture! in a sheet of flame
I saw them and I knew them all. And yet
Dauntless the slug-horn to my lips I set,
  And blew. '*Childe Roland to the Dark Tower came.*'

The Raven

Edgar Allan Poe

First published in the New York newspaper the *Evening Mirror*, 29 January 1845, under Poe's pseudonym, Quarles

ONCE upon a midnight dreary, while I pondered, weak and weary,
Over many a quaint and curious volume of forgotten lore –
While I nodded, nearly napping, suddenly there came a tapping,
As of someone gently rapping, rapping at my chamber door.
''Tis some visitor,' I muttered, 'tapping at my chamber door –
Only this and nothing more.'

Ah, distinctly I remember it was in the bleak December;
And each separate dying ember wrought its ghost upon the floor.
Eagerly I wished the morrow; vainly I had sought to borrow
From my books surcease of sorrow – sorrow for the lost Lenore –
For the rare and radiant maiden whom the angels name Lenore –
Nameless *here* for evermore.

And the silken, sad, uncertain rustling of each purple curtain
Thrilled me – filled me with fantastic terrors never felt before;
So that now, to still the beating of my heart, I stood repeating,
''Tis some visitor entreating entrance at my chamber door –

Some late visitor entreating entrance at my chamber door –
This it is and nothing more.'

Presently my soul grew stronger; hesitating then no longer,
'Sir,' said I, 'or Madam, truly your forgiveness I implore;
But the fact is I was napping, and so gently you came rapping,
And so faintly you came tapping, tapping at my chamber door,
That I scarce was sure I heard you' – here I opened wide the door –
Darkness there and nothing more.

Deep into that darkness peering, long I stood there wondering, fearing,
Doubting, dreaming dreams no mortal ever dared to dream before;
But the silence was unbroken, and the stillness gave no token,
And the only word there spoken was the whispered word, 'Lenore?'
This I whispered, and an echo murmured the word, 'Lenore!'
Merely this and nothing more.

Back into the chamber turning, all my soul within me burning,
Soon again I heard a tapping somewhat louder than before.
'Surely,' said I, 'surely that is something at my window lattice;
Let me see, then, what thereat is, and this mystery explore –
Let my heart be still a moment and this mystery explore –
'Tis the wind and nothing more!'

Open here I flung the shutter, when, with many a flirt and flutter,
In there stepped a stately Raven of the saintly days of yore;
Not the least obeisance made he; not a minute stopped or stayed he;

But, with mien of lord or lady, perched above my chamber
door –
Perched upon a bust of Pallas just above my chamber door –
Perched, and sat, and nothing more.

Then this ebony bird beguiling my sad fancy into smiling,
By the grave and stern decorum of the countenance it wore,
'Though thy crest be shorn and shaven, thou,' I said, 'art sure
no craven,
Ghastly grim and ancient Raven wandering from the Nightly
shore –
Tell me what thy lordly name is on the Night's Plutonian
shore!'
Quoth the Raven, 'Nevermore.'

Much I marvelled this ungainly fowl to hear discourse so
plainly,
Though its answer little meaning – little relevancy bore;
For we cannot help agreeing that no living human being
Ever yet was blessed with seeing bird above his chamber door –
Bird or beast upon the sculptured bust above his chamber door,
With such name as 'Nevermore.'

But the Raven, sitting lonely on the placid bust, spoke only
That one word, as if his soul in that one word he did outpour.
Nothing farther then he uttered – not a feather then he
fluttered –
Till I scarcely more than muttered, 'Other friends have flown
before –
On the morrow *he* will leave me, as my Hopes have flown
before.'
Then the bird said, 'Nevermore.'

Startled at the stillness broken by reply so aptly spoken,
'Doubtless,' said I, 'what it utters is its only stock and store
Caught from some unhappy master whom unmerciful Disaster
Followed fast and followed faster till his songs one burden
bore –
Till the dirges of his Hope that melancholy burden bore
Of "Never – nevermore."'

But the Raven still beguiling my sad fancy into smiling,
Straight I wheeled a cushioned seat in front of bird and bust
and door;
Then, upon the velvet sinking, I betook myself to linking
Fancy unto fancy, thinking what this ominous bird of yore –
What this grim, ungainly, ghastly, gaunt, and ominous bird of
yore
Meant in croaking 'Nevermore.'

This I sat engaged in guessing, but no syllable expressing
To the fowl whose fiery eyes now burned into my bosom's core;
This and more I sat divining, with my head at ease reclining
On the cushion's velvet lining that the lamplight gloated o'er,
But whose velvet-violet lining with the lamplight gloating o'er,
She shall press, ah, nevermore!

Then, methought, the air grew denser, perfumed from an
unseen censer
Swung by seraphim whose footfalls tinkled on the tufted floor.
'Wretch,' I cried, 'thy God hath lent thee – by these angels he
hath sent thee
Respite – respite and nepenthe from thy memories of Lenore;
Quaff, oh quaff this kind nepenthe and forget this lost Lenore!'
Quoth the Raven, 'Nevermore.'

'Prophet!' said I, 'thing of evil! – prophet still, if bird or devil! –
Whether Tempter sent, or whether tempest tossed thee here
ashore,
Desolate yet all undaunted, on this desert land enchanted –
On this home by Horror haunted – tell me truly, I implore –
Is there – *is* there balm in Gilead? – tell me – tell me, I
implore!'
Quoth the Raven, 'Nevermore.'

'Prophet!' said I, 'thing of evil! – prophet still, if bird or devil!
By that Heaven that bends above us – by that God we both
adore –
Tell this soul with sorrow laden if, within the distant Aidenn,
It shall clasp a sainted maiden whom the angels name Lenore –
Clasp a rare and radiant maiden whom the angels name
Lenore.'
Quoth the Raven, 'Nevermore.'

'Be that word our sign of parting, bird or fiend!' I shrieked,
upstarting –
'Get thee back into the tempest and the Night's Plutonian
shore!
Leave no black plume as a token of that lie thy soul hath
spoken!
Leave my loneliness unbroken! – quit the bust above my door!
Take thy beak from out my heart, and take thy form from off
my door!'
Quoth the Raven, 'Nevermore.'

And the Raven, never flitting, still is sitting, *still* is sitting
On the pallid bust of Pallas just above my chamber door;
And his eyes have all the seeming of a demon's that is dreaming,

And the lamplight o'er him streaming throws his shadow on the
floor;
And my soul from out that shadow that lies floating on the floor
Shall be lifted – nevermore!

The Wreck of the Hesperus

Henry Wadsworth Longfellow

First published in the magazine *The New World*, January 1840, about an event in 1839

It was the schooner Hesperus,
  That sailed the wintry sea;
And the skipper had taken his little daughter,
  To bear him company.

Blue were her eyes as the fairy-flax,
  Her cheeks like the dawn of day,
And her bosom white as the hawthorn buds
  That ope in the month of May.

The skipper he stood beside the helm,
  His pipe was in his mouth,
And he watched how the veering flaw did blow
  The smoke now west, now south.

Then up and spake an old sailor,
  Had sailed the Spanish Main,
'I pray thee, put into yonder port,
  For I fear a hurricane.

'Last night the moon had a golden ring,
  And tonight no moon we see!'
The skipper he blew a whiff from his pipe,
  And a scornful laugh laughed he.

Colder and louder blew the wind,
  A gale from the north-east,
The snow fell hissing in the brine,
  And the billows frothed like yeast.

Down came the storm, and smote amain
  The vessel in its strength;
She shuddered and paused, like a frighted steed,
  Then leaped her cable's length.

'Come hither! come hither! my little daughter,
  And do not tremble so;
For I can weather the roughest gale
  That ever wind did blow.'

He wrapped her warm in his seaman's coat
  Against the stinging blast;
He cut a rope from a broken spar,
  And bound her to the mast.

'O father! I hear the church bells ring,
  O say, what may it be?'
''Tis a fog-bell on a rock-bound coast!' –
  And he steered for the open sea.

'O father! I hear the sound of guns,
  O say, what may it be?'
'Some ship in distress, that cannot live
  In such an angry sea!'

'O father! I see a gleaming light,
O say, what may it be?'
But the father answered never a word,
A frozen corpse was he.

Lashed to the helm, all stiff and stark,
With his face turned to the skies,
The lantern gleamed through the gleaming snow
On his fixed and glassy eyes.

Then the maiden clasped her hands and prayed
That savèd she might be;
And she thought of Christ, who stilled the wave
On the Lake of Galilee.

And fast through the midnight dark and drear,
Through the whistling sleet and snow,
Like a sheeted ghost the vessel swept
Towards the reef of Norman's Woe.

And ever the fitful gusts between
A sound came from the land;
It was the sound of the trampling surf
On the rocks and the hard sea-sand.

The breakers were right beneath her bows,
She drifted a dreary wreck,
And a whooping billow swept the crew
Like icicles from her deck.

She struck where the white and fleecy waves
  Looked soft as carded wool,
But the cruel rocks they gored her side
  Like the horns of an angry bull.

Her rattling shrouds, all sheathed in ice,
  With the masts went by the board;
Like a vessel of glass she stove and sank –
  Ho! ho! the breakers roared!

At daybreak on the bleak sea-beach
  A fisherman stood aghast,
To see the form of a maiden fair
  Lashed close to a drifting mast.

The salt sea was frozen on her breast,
  The salt tears in her eyes;
And he saw her hair, like the brown sea-weed,
  On the billows fall and rise.

Such was the wreck of the Hesperus,
  In the midnight and the snow!
Christ save us all from a death like this,
  On the reef of Norman's Woe!

The Song of Hiawatha (abridged)

Henry Wadsworth Longfellow

First published as a separate book in 1855

INTRODUCTION

Should you ask me, whence these stories?
Whence these legends and traditions,
With the odours of the forest,
With the dew and damp of meadows,
With the curling smoke of wigwams,
With the rushing of great rivers,
With their frequent repetitions,
And their wild reverberations,
As of thunder in the mountains?
  I should answer, I should tell you,
'From the forests and the prairies,
From the great lakes of the North-land,
From the land of the Ojibways,
From the land of the Dacotahs,
From the mountains, moors, and fenlands,
Where the heron, the Shuh-shuh-gah,
Feeds among the reeds and rushes.
I repeat them as I heard them
From the lips of Nawadaha,
The musician, the sweet singer.'
  Should you ask where Nawadaha
Found these songs, so wild and wayward,
Found these legends and traditions,

I should answer, I should tell you,
'In the birds'-nests of the forest,
In the lodges of the beaver,
In the hoof-prints of the bison,
In the eyrie of the eagle!
'All the wild-fowl sang them to him,
In the moorlands and the fenlands,
In the melancholy marshes;
Chetowaik, the plover, sang them,
Mahng, the loon, the wild-goose, Wawa,
The blue heron, the Shuh-shuh-gah,
And the grouse, the Mushkodasa!'
If still further you should ask me,
Saying, 'Who was Nawadaha?
Tell us of this Nawadaha,'
I should answer your inquiries
Straightway in such words as follow.
'In the Vale of Tawasentha,
In the green and silent valley,
By the pleasant water-courses,
Dwelt the singer Nawadaha.
Round about the Indian village
Spread the meadows and the cornfields,
And beyond them stood the forest,
Stood the groves of singing pine-trees,
Green in Summer, white in Winter,
Ever sighing, ever singing.
'And the pleasant water-courses,
You could trace them through the valley,
By the rushing in the Spring-time,
By the alders in the Summer,
By the white fog in the Autumn,
By the black line in the Winter;

And beside them dwelt the singer,
In the Vale of Tawasentha,
In the green and silent valley.
'There he sang of Hiawatha,
Sang the Song of Hiawatha,
Sang his wondrous birth and being,
How he prayed and how he fasted,
How he lived, and toiled, and suffered,
That the tribes of men might prosper,
That he might advance his people!'

THE PEACE-PIPE

On the Mountains of the Prairie,
On the great Red Pipe-stone Quarry,
Gitche Manito, the mighty,
He the Master of Life, descending,
On the red crags of the quarry
Stood erect, and called the nations,
Called the tribes of men together.
From his footprints flowed a river,
Leaped into the light of morning,
O'er the precipice plunging downward
Gleamed like Ishkoodah, the comet.
And the Spirit, stooping earthward,
With his finger on the meadow
Traced a winding pathway for it,
Saying to it, 'Run in this way!'
From the red stone of the quarry
With his hand he broke a fragment,
Moulded it into a pipe-head,
Shaped and fashioned it with figures;
From the margin of the river
Took a long reed for a pipe-stem,

With its dark green leaves upon it;
Filled the pipe with bark of willow,
With the bark of the red willow;
Breathed upon the neighbouring forest,
Made its great boughs chafe together,
Till in flame they burst and kindled;
And erect upon the mountains,
Gitche Manito, the mighty,
Smoked the calumet, the Peace-Pipe,
As a signal to the nations.
And the smoke rose slowly, slowly,
Through the tranquil air of morning, –
First a single line of darkness,
Then a denser, bluer vapour,
Then a snow-white cloud unfolding,
Like the tree-tops of the forest,
Ever rising, rising, rising,
Till it touched the top of heaven,
Till it broke against the heaven,
And rolled outward all around it.
From the Vale of Tawasentha,
From the Valley of Wyoming,
From the groves of Tuscaloosa,
From the far-off Rocky Mountains,
From the Northern lakes and rivers
All the tribes beheld the signal,
Saw the distant smoke ascending,
The Pukwana of the Peace-Pipe.
And the Prophets of the nations
Said: 'Behold it, the Pukwana!
By this signal from afar off,
Bending like a wand of willow,
Waving like a hand that beckons,

Gitche Manito, the mighty,
Calls the tribes of men together,
Calls the warriors to his council!'
  Down the rivers, o'er the prairies,
Came the warriors of the nations,
Came the Delawares and Mohawks,
Came the Choctaws and Comanches,
Came the Shoshonies and Blackfeet,
Came the Pawnees and Omahas,
Came the Mandans and Dacotahs,
Came the Hurons and Ojibways,
All the warriors drawn together
By the signal of the Peace-Pipe,
To the Mountains of the Prairie,
To the great Red Pipe-stone Quarry.
  And they stood there on the meadow,
With their weapons and their war-gear,
Painted like the leaves of Autumn,
Painted like the sky of morning,
Wildly glaring at each other;
In their faces stern defiance,
In their hearts the feuds of ages,
The hereditary hatred,
The ancestral thirst of vengeance.
  Gitche Manito, the mighty,
The creator of the nations,
Looked upon them with compassion,
With paternal love and pity;
Looked upon their wrath and wrangling
But as quarrels among children,
But as feuds and fights of children!
  Over them he stretched his right hand,
To subdue their stubborn natures,

To allay their thirst and fever,
By the shadow of his right hand;
Spake to them with voice majestic
As the sound of far-off waters,
Falling into deep abysses,
Warning, chiding, spake in this wise: –
  'O my children! my poor children!
Listen to the words of wisdom,
Listen to the words of warning,
From the lips of the Great Spirit,
From the Master of Life, who made you.
  'I have given you lands to hunt in,
I have given you streams to fish in,
I have given you bear and bison,
I have given you roe and reindeer,
I have given you brant and beaver,
Filled the marshes full of wild-fowl,
Filled the rivers full of fishes;
Why then are you not contented?
Why then will you hunt each other?
  'I am weary of your quarrels,
Weary of your wars and bloodshed,
Weary of your prayers for vengeance,
Of your wranglings and dissensions;
All your strength is in your union,
All your danger is in discord;
Therefore be at peace henceforward,
And as brothers live together.
  'I will send a Prophet to you,
A Deliverer of the nations,
Who shall guide you and shall teach you,
Who shall toil and suffer with you.
If you listen to his counsels,

You will multiply and prosper;
If his warnings pass unheeded,
You will fade away and perish!
  'Bathe now in the stream before you,
Wash the war-paint from your faces,
Wash the blood-stains from your fingers,
Bury your war-clubs and your weapons,
Break the red stone from this quarry,
Mould and make it into Peace-Pipes,
Take the reeds that grow beside you,
Deck them with your brightest feathers,
Smoke the calumet together,
And as brothers live henceforward!'
  Then upon the ground the warriors
Threw their cloaks and shirts of deerskin,
Threw their weapons and their war-gear,
Leaped into the rushing river,
Washed the war-paint from their faces.
Clear above them flowed the water,
Clear and limpid from the footprints
Of the Master of Life descending;
Dark below them flowed the water,
Soiled and stained with streaks of crimson,
As if blood were mingled with it!
  From the river came the warriors,
Clean and washed from all their war-paint;
On the banks their clubs they buried,
Buried all their warlike weapons.
Gitche Manito, the mighty,
The Great Spirit, the creator,
Smiled upon his helpless children!
  And in silence all the warriors
Broke the red stone of the quarry,

Smoothed and formed it into Peace-Pipes,
Broke the long reeds by the river,
Decked them with their brightest feathers,
And departed each one homeward,
While the Master of Life, ascending,
Through the opening of cloud-curtains,
Through the doorways of the heaven,
Vanished from before their faces,
In the smoke that rolled around him,
The Pukwana of the Peace-Pipe!

HIAWATHA'S CHILDHOOD

DOWNWARD through the evening twilight,
In the days that are forgotten,
In the unremembered ages,
From the full moon fell Nokomis,
Fell the beautiful Nokomis,
She a wife, but not a mother.
  She was sporting with her women
Swinging in a swing of grape-vines,
When her rival, the rejected,
Full of jealousy and hatred,
Cut the leafy swing asunder,
Cut in twain the twisted grape-vines,
And Nokomis fell affrighted
Downward through the evening twilight,
On the Muskoday, the meadow,
On the prairie full of blossoms.
'See! a star falls!' said the people;
'From the sky a star is falling!'
  There among the ferns and mosses,
There among the prairie lilies,
On the Muskoday, the meadow,

In the moonlight and the starlight,
Fair Nokomis bore a daughter.
And she called her name Wenonah,
As the first-born of her daughters.
And the daughter of Nokomis
Grew up like the prairie lilies,
Grew a tall and slender maiden,
With the beauty of the moonlight,
With the beauty of the starlight.
  And Nokomis warned her often,
Saying oft, and oft repeating,
'O, beware of Mudjekeewis,
Of the West-Wind, Mudjekeewis;
Listen not to what he tells you;
Lie not down upon the meadow,
Stoop not down among the lilies,
Lest the West-Wind come and harm you!'
  But she heeded not the warning,
Heeded not those words of wisdom,
And the West-Wind came at evening,
Walking lightly o'er the prairie,
Whispering to the leaves and blossoms,
Bending low the flowers and grasses,
Found the beautiful Wenonah,
Lying there among the lilies,
Wooed her with his words of sweetness,
Wooed her with his soft caresses,
Till she bore a son in sorrow,
Bore a son of love and sorrow.
  Thus was born my Hiawatha,
Thus was born the child of wonder;
But the daughter of Nokomis,
Hiawatha's gentle mother,

In her anguish died deserted
By the West-Wind, false and faithless,
By the heartless Mudjekeewis.
  By the shores of Gitche Gumee
By the shining Big-Sea-Water,
Stood the wigwam of Nokomis,
Daughter of the Moon, Nokomis.
Dark behind it rose the forest,
Rose the black and gloomy pine-trees,
Rose the firs with cones upon them;
Bright before it beat the water,
Beat the clear and sunny water,
Beat the shining Big-Sea-Water.
  There the wrinkled, old Nokomis
Nursed the little Hiawatha,
Rocked him in his linden cradle,
Bedded soft in moss and rushes,
Safely bound with reindeer sinews;
Stilled his fretful wail by saying,
'Hush! the Naked Bear will hear thee!'
Lulled him into slumber, singing,
'Ewa-yea! my little owlet!
Who is this, that lights the wigwam?
With his great eyes lights the wigwam?
Ewa-yea! my little owlet!'
  Many things Nokomis taught him
Of the stars that shine in heaven;
Showed him Ishkoodah, the comet,
Ishkoodah, with fiery tresses;
Showed the Death-Dance of the spirits,
Warriors with their plumes and war-clubs,
Flaring far away to northward
In the frosty nights of Winter;

Showed the broad, white road in heaven,
Pathway of the ghosts, the shadows,
Running straight across the heavens,
Crowded with the ghosts, the shadows.
  At the door on summer evenings
Sat the little Hiawatha;
Heard the whispering of the pine-trees,
Heard the lapping of the water,
Sounds of music, words of wonder;
'Minne-wawa!' said the pine-trees,
'Mudway-aushka!' said the water.
  Saw the fire-fly, Wah-wah-taysee,
Flitting through the dusk of evening,
With the twinkle of its candle
Lighting up the brakes and bushes;
And he sang the song of children,
Sang the song Nokomis taught him:
'Wah-wah-taysee, little fire-fly,
Little, flitting, white-fire insect,
Little, dancing, white-fire creature,
Light me with your little candle,
Ere upon my bed I lay me,
Ere in sleep I close my eyelids!'
  Saw the moon rise from the water
Rippling, rounding from the water,
Saw the flecks and shadows on it,
Whispered, 'What is that, Nokomis?'
And the good Nokomis answered:
'Once a warrior, very angry,
Seized his grandmother, and threw her
Up into the sky at midnight;
Right against the moon he threw her;
'Tis her body that you see there.'

Saw the rainbow in the heaven,
In the eastern sky, the rainbow,
Whispered, 'What is that, Nokomis?'
And the good Nokomis answered:
''Tis the heaven of flowers you see there;
All the wild-flowers of the forest,
All the lilies of the prairie,
When on earth they fade and perish,
Blossom in that heaven above us.'
When he heard the owls at midnight,
Hooting, laughing in the forest,
'What is that?' he cried in terror;
'What is that?' he said, 'Nokomis?'
And the good Nokomis answered:
'That is but the owl and owlet,
Talking in their native language,
Talking, scolding at each other.'
Then the little Hiawatha
Learned of every bird its language,
Learned their names and all their secrets,
How they built their nests in Summer,
Where they hid themselves in Winter,
Talked with them whene'er he met them,
Called them 'Hiawatha's Chickens.'
Of all beasts he learned the language,
Learned their names and all their secrets,
How the beavers built their lodges,
Where the squirrels hid their acorns,
How the reindeer ran so swiftly,
Why the rabbit was so timid,
Talked with them whene'er he met them,
Called them 'Hiawatha's Brothers.'
Then Iagoo, the great boaster,

He the marvellous story-teller,
He the traveller and the talker,
He the friend of old Nokomis,
Made a bow for Hiawatha;
From a branch of ash he made it,
From an oak-bough made the arrows,
Tipped with flint, and winged with feathers,
And the cord he made of deerskin.
   Then he said to Hiawatha:
'Go, my son, into the forest,
Where the red deer herd together,
Kill for us a famous roebuck,
Kill for us a deer with antlers!'
   Forth into the forest straightway
All alone walked Hiawatha
Proudly, with his bow and arrows;
And the birds sang round him, o'er him,
'Do not shoot us, Hiawatha!'
Sang the robin, the Opechee,
Sang the bluebird, the Owaissa,
'Do not shoot us, Hiawatha!'
   Up the oak-tree, close beside him,
Sprang the squirrel, Adjidaumo,
In and out among the branches,
Coughed and chattered from the oak-tree,
Laughed, and said between his laughing,
'Do not shoot me, Hiawatha!'
   And the rabbit from his pathway
Leaped aside, and at a distance
Sat erect upon his haunches,
Half in fear and half in frolic,
Saying to the little hunter,
'Do not shoot me, Hiawatha!'

But he heeded not, nor heard them,
For his thoughts were with the red deer;
On their tracks his eyes were fastened,
Leading downward to the river,
To the ford across the river,
And as one in slumber walked he.

Hidden in the alder-bushes,
There he waited till the deer came,
Till he saw two antlers lifted,
Saw two eyes look from the thicket,
Saw two nostrils point to windward,
And a deer came down the pathway,
Flecked with leafy light and shadow.
And his heart within him fluttered,
Trembled like the leaves above him,
Like the birch-leaf palpitated,
As the deer came down the pathway.

Then, upon one knee uprising,
Hiawatha aimed an arrow;
Scarce a twig moved with his motion,
Scarce a leaf was stirred or rustled;
But the wary roebuck started,
Stamped with all his hoofs together,
Listened with one foot uplifted,
Leaped as if to meet the arrow;
Ah! the singing, fatal arrow,
Like a wasp it buzzed and stung him!

Dead he lay there in the forest,
By the ford across the river;
Beat his timid heart no longer,
But the heart of Hiawatha
Throbbed and shouted and exulted,
As he bore the red deer homeward

And Iagoo and Nokomis
Hailed his coming with applauses.
From the red deer's hide Nokomis
Made a cloak for Hiawatha,
From the red deer's flesh Nokomis
Made a banquet in his honour.
All the village came and feasted,
All the guests praised Hiawatha,
Called him Strong-Heart, Soan-ge-taha!
Called him Loon-Heart, Mahn-go-taysee!

HIAWATHA AND MUDJEKEEWIS

Out of childhood into manhood
Now had grown my Hiawatha,
Skilled in all the craft of hunters,
Learned in all the lore of old men,
In all youthful sports and pastimes,
In all manly arts and labours.
Swift of foot was Hiawatha;
He could shoot an arrow from him,
And run forward with such fleetness,
That the arrow fell behind him!
Strong of arm was Hiawatha;
He could shoot ten arrows upward,
Shoot them with such strength and swiftness,
That the tenth had left the bowstring
Ere the first to earth had fallen!
He had mittens, Minjekahwun,
Magic mittens made of deerskin;
When upon his hands he wore them,
He could smite the rocks asunder,
He could grind them into powder.
He had moccasins enchanted,

Magic moccasins of deerskin;
When he bound them round his ankles,
When upon his feet he tied them,
At each stride a mile he measured!
  Much he questioned old Nokomis
Of his father Mudjekeewis;
Learned from her the fatal secret
Of the beauty of his mother,
Of the falsehood of his father;
And his heart was hot within him,
Like a living coal his heart was.
  Then he said to old Nokomis,
'I will go to Mudjekeewis,
See how fares it with my father,
At the doorways of the West-Wind,
At the portals of the Sunset!'
  Warning said the old Nokomis,
'Go not forth, O Hiawatha!
To the kingdom of the West-Wind,
To the realms of Mudjekeewis,
Lest he harm you with his magic,
Lest he kill you with his cunning!'
  But the fearless Hiawatha
Heeded not her woman's warning;
Forth he strode into the forest,
At each stride a mile he measured;
Lurid seemed the sky above him,
Lurid seemed the earth beneath him,
Hot and close the air around him,
Filled with smoke and fiery vapours,
As of burning woods and prairies,
For his heart was hot within him,
Like a living coal his heart was.

So he journeyed westward, westward,
Left the fleetest deer behind him,
Left the antelope and bison;
Crossed the rushing Esconaba,
Crossed the mighty Mississippi,
Passed the Mountains of the Prairie,
Passed the land of Crows and Foxes,
Passed the dwellings of the Blackfeet,
Came unto the Rocky Mountains,
To the kingdom of the West-Wind,
Where upon the gusty summits
Sat the ancient Mudjekeewis,
Ruler of the winds of heaven.

Filled with awe was Hiawatha
At the aspect of his father.
On the air about him wildly
Tossed and streamed his cloudy tresses,
Gleamed like drifting snow his tresses,
Glared like Ishkoodah, the comet,
Like the star with fiery tresses.

Filled with joy was Mudjekeewis
When he looked on Hiawatha,
Saw his youth rise up before him
In the face of Hiawatha,
Saw the beauty of Wenonah
From the grave rise up before him.

'Welcome!' said he, 'Hiawatha,
To the kingdom of the West-Wind!
Long have I been waiting for you!
Youth is lovely, age is lonely,
Youth is fiery, age is frosty;
You bring back the days departed,
You bring back my youth of passion,

And the beautiful Wenonah!'
  Many days they talked together,
Questioned, listened, waited, answered;
Much the mighty Mudjekeewis
Boasted of his ancient prowess,
Of his perilous adventures,
His indomitable courage,
His invulnerable body.
  Patiently sat Hiawatha,
Listening to his father's boasting;
With a smile he sat and listened,
Uttered neither threat nor menace,
Neither word nor look betrayed him;
But his heart was hot within him,
Like a living coal his heart was.
  Then he said, 'O Mudjekeewis,
Is there nothing that can harm you?
Nothing that you are afraid of?'
And the mighty Mudjekeewis,
Grand and gracious in his boasting,
Answered, saying, 'There is nothing,
Nothing but the black rock yonder,
Nothing but the fatal Wawbeek!'
  And he looked at Hiawatha
With a wise look and benignant,
With a countenance paternal,
Looked with pride upon the beauty
Of his tall and graceful figure,
Saying, 'O my Hiawatha!
Is there anything can harm you?
Anything you are afraid of?'
  But the wary Hiawatha
Paused awhile, as if uncertain,

Held his peace, as if resolving,
And then answered, 'There is nothing,
Nothing but the bulrush yonder,
Nothing but the great Apukwa!'
Then they talked of other matters;
First of Hiawatha's brothers,
First of Wabun, of the East-Wind,
Of the South-Wind, Shawondasee,
Of the North, Kabibonokka;
Then of Hiawatha's mother,
Of the beautiful Wenonah,
Of her birth upon the meadow,
Of her death, as old Nokomis
Had remembered and related.
And he cried, 'O Mudjekeewis,
It was you who killed Wenonah,
Took her young life and her beauty,
Broke the Lily of the Prairie,
Trampled it beneath your footsteps;
You confess it! you confess it!'
And the mighty Mudjekeewis
Tossed upon the wind his tresses,
Bowed his hoary head in anguish,
With a silent nod assented.
Then upstarted Hiawatha,
And with threatening look and gesture
Laid his hand upon the black rock,
On the fatal Wawbeek laid it,
With his mittens, Minjekahwun,
Rent the jutting crag asunder,
Smote and crushed it into fragments,
Hurled them madly at his father,
The remorseful Mudjekeewis;

For his heart was hot within him,
Like a living coal his heart was.
  But the ruler of the West-Wind
Blew the fragments backward from him,
With the breathing of his nostrils,
With the tempest of his anger,
Blew them back at his assailant;
Seized the bulrush, the Apukwa,
Dragged it with its roots and fibres
From the margin of the meadow,
From its ooze, the giant bulrush;
Long and loud laughed Hiawatha!
  Then began the deadly conflict,
Hand to hand among the mountains;
From his eyrie screamed the eagle,
The Keneu, the great war-eagle;
Sat upon the crags around them,
Wheeling flapped his wings above them.
  Like a tall tree in the tempest
Bent and lashed the giant bulrush;
And in masses huge and heavy
Crashing fell the fatal Wawbeek;
Till the earth shook with the tumult
And confusion of the battle,
And the air was full of shoutings,
And the thunder of the mountains,
Starting, answered, 'Baim-wawa!'
  Back retreated Mudjekeewis,
Rushing westward o'er the mountains,
Stumbling westward down the mountains,
Three whole days retreated fighting,
Still pursued by Hiawatha
To the doorways of the West-Wind,

To the portals of the Sunset,
To the earth's remotest border,
Where into the empty spaces
Sinks the sun, as a flamingo
Drops into her nest at nightfall,
In the melancholy marshes.
'Hold!' at length cried Mudjekeewis,
'Hold, my son, my Hiawatha!
'Tis impossible to kill me,
For you cannot kill the immortal,
I have put you to this trial,
But to know and prove your courage;
Now receive the prize of valour!
'Go back to your home and people,
Live among them, toil among them,
Cleanse the earth from all that harms it,
Clear the fishing-grounds and rivers,
Slay all monsters and magicians,
All the Wendigoes, the giants,
All the serpents, the Kenabeeks,
As I slew the Mishe-Mokwa,
Slew the Great Bear of the mountains.
'And at last when Death draws near you,
When the awful eyes of Pauguk
Glare upon you in the darkness,
I will share my kingdom with you;
Ruler shall you be thenceforward
Of the Northwest-Wind, Keewaydin,
Of the home-wind, the Keewaydin.'
Thus was fought that famous battle
In the dreadful days of Shah-shah,
In the days long since departed,
In the kingdom of the West-Wind.

Still the hunter sees its traces
Scattered far o'er hill and valley;
Sees the giant bulrush growing
By the ponds and water-courses,
Sees the masses of the Wawbeek
Lying still in every valley.
  Homeward now went Hiawatha;
Pleasant was the landscape round him,
Pleasant was the air above him,
For the bitterness of anger
Had departed wholly from him,
From his brain the thought of vengeance,
From his heart the burning fever.
  Only once his pace he slackened,
Only once he paused or halted,
Paused to purchase heads of arrows
Of the ancient Arrow-maker,
In the land of the Dacotahs,
Where the Falls of Minnehaha
Flash and gleam among the oak-trees,
Laugh and leap into the valley.
  There the ancient Arrow-maker
Made his arrow-heads of sandstone,
Arrow-heads of chalcedony,
Arrow-heads of flint and jasper,
Smoothed and sharpened at the edges,
Hard and polished, keen and costly.
  With him dwelt his dark-eyed daughter,
Wayward as the Minnehaha,
With her moods of shade and sunshine,
Eyes that smiled and frowned alternate,
Feet as rapid as the river,
Tresses flowing like the water,

And as musical a laughter;
And he named her from the river,
From the waterfall he named her,
Minnehaha, Laughing Water.
Was it then for heads of arrows,
Arrow-heads of chalcedony,
Arrow-heads of flint and jasper,
That my Hiawatha halted
In the land of the Dacotahs?
Was it not to see the maiden,
See the face of Laughing Water
Peeping from behind the curtain,
Hear the rustling of her garments
From behind the waving curtain,
As one sees the Minnehaha
Gleaming, glancing through the branches,
As one hears the Laughing Water
From behind its screen of branches?
Who shall say what thoughts and visions
Fill the fiery brains of young men?
Who shall say what dreams of beauty
Filled the heart of Hiawatha?
All he told to old Nokomis,
When he reached the lodge at sunset,
Was the meeting with his father,
Was his fight with Mudjekeewis;
Not a word he said of arrows,
Not a word of Laughing Water.

HIAWATHA'S FRIENDS

Two good friends had Hiawatha,
Singled out from all the others,
Bound to him in closest union,

And to whom he gave the right hand
Of his heart, in joy and sorrow;
Chibiabos, the musician,
And the very strong man, Kwasind.
  Most beloved by Hiawatha
Was the gentle Chibiabos,
He the best of all musicians,
He the sweetest of all singers.
Beautiful and childlike was he,
Brave as man is, soft as woman,
Pliant as a wand of willow,
Stately as a deer with antlers.
  When he sang, the village listened;
All the warriors gathered round him,
All the women came to hear him;
Now he stirred their souls to passion,
Now he melted them to pity.
  From the hollow reeds he fashioned
Flutes so musical and mellow,
That the brook, the Sebowisha,
Ceased to murmur in the woodland,
That the wood-birds ceased from singing,
And the squirrel, Adjidaumo,
Ceased his chatter in the oak-tree,
And the rabbit, the Wabasso,
Sat upright to look and listen.
  All the many sounds of nature
Borrowed sweetness from his singing;
All the hearts of men were softened
By the pathos of his music;
For he sang of peace and freedom,
Sang of beauty, love, and longing;
Sang of death, and life undying

In the Islands of the Blessed,
In the kingdom of Ponemah,
In the land of the Hereafter.
  Very dear to Hiawatha
Was the gentle Chibiabos,
He the best of all musicians,
He the sweetest of all singers;
For his gentleness he loved him,
And the magic of his singing.
  Dear, too, unto Hiawatha
Was the very strong man, Kwasind,
He the strongest of all mortals,
He the mightiest among many;
For his very strength he loved him,
For his strength allied to goodness.
  Once as down that foaming river,
Down the rapids of Pauwating,
Kwasind sailed with his companions,
In the stream he saw a beaver,
Saw Ahmeek, the King of Beavers,
Struggling with the rushing currents,
Rising, sinking in the water.
  Without speaking, without pausing,
Kwasind leaped into the river,
Plunged beneath the bubbling surface,
Through the whirlpools chased the beaver,
Followed him among the islands,
Stayed so long beneath the water,
That his terrified companions
Cried, 'Alas! good-bye to Kwasind!
We shall never more see Kwasind!'
But he reappeared triumphant,
And upon his shining shoulders

Brought the beaver, dead and dripping,
Brought the King of all the Beavers.
  And these two, as I have told you,
Were the friends of Hiawatha,
Chibiabos, the musician,
And the very strong man, Kwasind.
Long they lived in peace together,
Spake with naked hearts together,
Pondering much and much contriving
How the tribes of men might prosper.

HIAWATHA'S WOOING

'As unto the bow the cord is,
So unto the man is woman,
Though she bends him, she obeys him,
Though she draws him, yet she follows,
Useless each without the other!'
  Thus the youthful Hiawatha
Said within himself and pondered,
Much perplexed by various feelings,
Listless, longing, hoping, fearing,
Dreaming still of Minnehaha,
Of the lovely Laughing Water,
In the land of the Dacotahs.
  'Wed a maiden of your people,'
Warning said the old Nokomis;
'Go not eastward, go not westward,
For a stranger, whom we know not!
Like a fire upon the hearthstone
Is a neighbour's homely daughter;
Like the starlight or the moonlight
Is the handsomest of strangers!'
  Thus dissuading spake Nokomis,

And my Hiawatha answered
Only this: 'Dear old Nokomis,
Very pleasant is the firelight,
But I like the starlight better,
Better do I like the moonlight!'
  Gravely then said old Nokomis:
'Bring not here an idle maiden,
Bring not here a useless woman,
Hands unskilful, feet unwilling;
Bring a wife with nimble fingers,
Heart and hand that move together,
Feet that run on willing errands!'
  Smiling answered Hiawatha:
'In the land of the Dacotahs
Lives the Arrow-maker's daughter,
Minnehaha, Laughing Water,
Handsomest of all the women.
I will bring her to your wigwam,
She shall run upon your errands,
Be your starlight, moonlight, firelight,
Be the sunlight of my people!'
  Still dissuading said Nokomis:
'Bring not to my lodge a stranger
From the land of the Dacotahs!
Very fierce are the Dacotahs,
Often is there war between us,
There are feuds yet unforgotten,
Wounds that ache and still may open!'
  Laughing answered Hiawatha:
'For that reason, if no other,
Would I wed the fair Dacotah,
That our tribes might be united,
That old feuds might be forgotten,

And old wounds be healed for ever!'
  Thus departed Hiawatha
To the land of the Dacotahs,
To the land of handsome women;
Striding over moor and meadow,
Through interminable forests,
Through uninterrupted silence.
  With his moccasins of magic,
At each stride a mile he measured;
Yet the way seemed long before him,
And his heart outran his footsteps;
And he journeyed without resting,
Till he heard the cataract's laughter,
Heard the Falls of Minnehaha
Calling to him through the silence.
'Pleasant is the sound!' he murmured,
'Pleasant is the voice that calls me!'
  On the outskirts of the forest,
'Twixt the shadow and the sunshine,
Herds of fallow deer were feeding,
But they saw not Hiawatha;
To his bow he whispered, 'Fail not!'
To his arrow whispered, 'Swerve not!'
Sent it singing on its errand,
To the red heart of the roebuck;
Threw the deer across his shoulder,
And sped forward without pausing.
  At the doorway of his wigwam
Sat the ancient Arrow-maker,
In the land of the Dacotahs,
Making arrow-heads of jasper,
Arrow-heads of chalcedony.
At his side, in all her beauty,

Sat the lovely Minnehaha,
Sat his daughter, Laughing Water,
Plaiting mats of flags and rushes;
Of the past the old man's thoughts were,
And the maiden's of the future.
  He was thinking, as he sat there,
Of the days when with such arrows
He had struck the deer and bison,
On the Muskoday, the meadow;
Shot the wildgoose, flying southward,
On the wing, the clamorous Wawa;
Thinking of the great war-parties,
How they came to buy his arrows,
Could not fight without his arrows.
Ah, no more such noble warriors
Could be found on earth as they were!
Now the men were all like women,
Only used their tongues for weapons!
  She was thinking of a hunter,
From another tribe and country,
Young and tall and very handsome,
Who one morning in the Spring-time
Came to buy her father's arrows,
Sat and rested in the wigwam,
Lingered long about the doorway,
Looking back as he departed.
She had heard her father praise him,
Praise his courage and his wisdom;
Would he come again for arrows
To the Falls of Minnehaha?
On the mat her hands lay idle,
And her eyes were very dreamy.
  Through their thoughts they heard a footstep,

Heard a rustling in the branches,
And with glowing cheek and forehead,
With the deer upon his shoulders,
Suddenly from out the woodlands
Hiawatha stood before them.
  Straight the ancient Arrow-maker
Looked up gravely from his labour,
Laid aside the unfinished arrow,
Bade him enter at the doorway,
Saying, as he rose to meet him,
'Hiawatha, you are welcome!'
  At the feet of Laughing Water
Hiawatha laid his burden,
Threw the red deer from his shoulders;
And the maiden looked up at him,
Looked up from her mat of rushes,
Said with gentle look and accent,
'You are welcome, Hiawatha!'
  Then uprose the Laughing Water,
From the ground fair Minnehaha,
Laid aside her mat unfinished,
Brought forth food and set before them,
Water brought them from the brooklet,
Gave them food in earthen vessels,
Gave them drink in bowls of bass-wood,
Listened while the guest was speaking,
Listened while her father answered;
But not once her lips she opened,
Not a single word she uttered.
  Yes, as in a dream she listened
To the words of Hiawatha,
As he talked of old Nokomis,
Who had nursed him in his childhood,

As he told of his companions,
Chibiabos, the musician,
And the very strong man, Kwasind,
And of happiness and plenty
In the land of the Ojibways,
In the pleasant land and peaceful.
'After many years of warfare,
Many years of strife and bloodshed,
There is peace between the Ojibways
And the tribe of the Dacotahs.'
Thus continued Hiawatha,
And then added, speaking slowly,
'That this peace may last for ever,
And our hands be clasped more closely,
And our hearts be more united,
Give me as my wife this maiden,
Minnehaha, Laughing Water,
Loveliest of Dacotah women!'
And the ancient Arrow-maker
Paused a moment ere he answered,
Smoked a little while in silence,
Looked at Hiawatha proudly,
Fondly looked at Laughing Water,
And made answer very gravely:
'Yes, if Minnehaha wishes;
Let your heart speak, Minnehaha!'
And the lovely Laughing Water
Seemed more lovely, as she stood there,
Neither willing nor reluctant,
As she went to Hiawatha,
Softly took the seat beside him,
While she said, and blushed to say it,
'I will follow you, my husband!'

This was Hiawatha's wooing!
Thus it was he won the daughter
Of the ancient Arrow-maker,
In the land of the Dacotahs!
From the wigwam he departed,
Leading with him Laughing Water;
Hand in hand they went together,
Through the woodland and the meadow,
Left the old man standing lonely
At the doorway of his wigwam,
Heard the Falls of Minnehaha
Calling to them from the distance,
Crying to them from afar off,
'Fare thee well, O Minnehaha!'
And the ancient Arrow-maker
Turned again unto his labour,
Sat down by his sunny doorway,
Murmuring to himself, and saying:
'Thus it is our daughters leave us,
Those we love, and those who love us!
Just when they have learned to help us,
When we are old and lean upon them,
Comes a youth with flaunting feathers,
With his flute of reeds, a stranger
Wanders piping through the village,
Beckons to the fairest maiden,
And she follows where he leads her,
Leaving all things for the stranger!'
Thus it was they journeyed homeward;
Thus it was that Hiawatha
To the lodge of old Nokomis
Brought the moonlight, starlight, firelight,
Brought the sunshine of his people,

Minnehaha, Laughing Water,
Handsomest of all the women
In the land of the Dacotahs,
In the land of handsome women.

BLESSING THE CORNFIELDS

SING, O Song of Hiawatha,
Of the happy days that followed,
In the land of the Ojibways,
In the pleasant land and peaceful!
Sing the mysteries of Mondamin,
Sing the Blessing of the Cornfields!
Buried was the bloody hatchet,
Buried was the dreadful war-club,
Buried were all warlike weapons,
And the war-cry was forgotten.
There was peace among the nations;
Unmolested roved the hunters,
Built the birch-canoe for sailing,
Caught the fish in lake and river,
Shot the deer and trapped the beaver;
Unmolested worked the women,
Made their sugar from the maple,
Gathered wild rice in the meadows,
Dressed the skins of deer and beaver.
All around the happy village
Stood the maize-fields, green and shining,
Waved the green plumes of Mondamin,
Waved his soft and sunny tresses,
Filling all the land with plenty.
'Twas the women who in Spring-time
Planted the broad fields and fruitful,
Buried in the earth Mondamin;

'Twas the women who in Autumn
Stripped the yellow husks of harvest,
Stripped the garments from Mondamin,
Even as Hiawatha taught them.

Once, when all the maize was planted,
Hiawatha, wise and thoughtful,
Spake and said to Minnehaha,
To his wife, the Laughing Water:
'You shall bless to-night the cornfields,
Draw a magic circle round them,
To protect them from destruction,
Blast of mildew, blight of insect,
Wagemin, the thief of cornfields,
Paimosaid, who steels the maize-ear!

'In the night, when all is silence,
In the night, when all is darkness,
When the Spirit of Sleep, Nepahwin,
Shuts the doors of all the wigwams,
So that not an ear can hear you,
So that not an eye can see you,
Rise up from your bed in silence,
Lay aside your garments wholly,
Walk around the fields you planted,
Round the borders of the cornfields,
Covered by your tresses only,
Robed with darkness as a garment.

'Thus the fields shall be more fruitful,
And the passing of your footsteps
Draw a magic circle round them,
So that neither blight nor mildew,
Neither burrowing worm nor insect,
Shall pass o'er the magic circle;
Not the dragon-fly, Kwo-neshe,

Nor the spider, Subbekashe,
Nor the grasshopper, Pah-puk-keena,
Nor the mighty caterpillar,
Way-muk-kwana, with the bearskin,
King of all the caterpillars!'
  On the tree-tops near the cornfields
Sat the hungry crows and ravens,
Kahgahgee, the King of Ravens,
With his band of black marauders.
And they laughed at Hiawatha,
Till the tree-tops shook with laughter,
With their melancholy laughter,
At the words of Hiawatha.
'Hear him!' said they; 'hear the Wise Man,
Hear the plots of Hiawatha!'
  When the noiseless night descended
Broad and dark o'er field and forest,
When the mournful Wawonaissa,
Sorrowing sang among the hemlocks,
And the Spirit of Sleep, Nepahwin,
Shut the doors of all the wigwams,
From her bed rose Laughing Water,
Laid aside her garments wholly,
And with darkness clothed and guarded,
Unashamed and unaffrighted,
Walked securely round the cornfields,
Drew the sacred magic circle
Of her footprints round the cornfields.
  No one but the Midnight only
Saw her beauty in the darkness;
No one but the Wawonaissa
Heard the panting of her bosom;
Guskewau, the darkness, wrapped her

Closely in his sacred mantle,
So that none might see her beauty,
So that none might boast, 'I saw her!'
  On the morrow, as the day dawned,
Kahgahgee, the King of Ravens,
Gathered all his black marauders,
Crows and blackbirds, jays and ravens,
Clamorous on the dusky tree-tops,
And descended, fast and fearless,
On the fields of Hiawatha,
On the grave of the Mondamin.
  'We will drag Mondamin,' said they,
'From the grave where he is buried,
Spite of all the magic circles
Laughing Water draws around it,
Spite of all the sacred footprints
Minnehaha stamps upon it!'
  But the wary Hiawatha,
Ever thoughtful, careful, watchful,
Had o'erheard the scornful laughter
When they mocked him from the tree-tops.
'Kaw!' he said, 'my friends the ravens!
Kahgahgee, my King of Ravens!
I will teach you all a lesson
That shall not be soon forgotten!'
  He had risen before the daybreak,
He had spread o'er all the cornfields
Snares to catch the black marauders,
And was lying now in ambush
In the neighbouring grove of pine-trees,
Waiting for the crows and blackbirds,
Waiting for the jays and ravens.
  Soon they came with caw and clamour,

Rush of wings and cry of voices,
To their work of devastation,
Settling down upon the cornfields,
Delving deep with beak and talon,
For the body of Mondamin.
And with all their craft and cunning,
All their skill in wiles of warfare,
They perceived no danger near them,
Till their claws became entangled,
Till they found themselves imprisoned
In the snares of Hiawatha.
From his place of ambush came he,
Striding terrible among them,
And so awful was his aspect
That the bravest quailed with terror.
Without mercy he destroyed them
Right and left, by tens and twenties,
And their wretched, lifeless bodies
Hung aloft on poles for scarecrows
Round the consecrated cornfields,
As a signal of his vengeance,
As a warning to marauders.
Only Kahgahgee, the leader,
Kahgahgee, the King of Ravens,
He alone was spared among them
As a hostage for his people.
With his prisoner-string he bound him,
Led him captive to his wigwam,
Tied him fast with cords of elm-bark
To the ridge-pole of his wigwam.
'Kahgahgee, my raven!' said he,
'You the leader of the robbers,
You the plotter of this mischief,

The contriver of this outrage,
I will keep you, I will hold you,
As a hostage for your people,
As a pledge of good behaviour!'
  And he left him, grim and sulky,
Sitting in the morning sunshine
On the summit of the wigwam,
Croaking fiercely his displeasure,
Flapping his great sable pinions,
Vainly struggling for his freedom,
Vainly calling on his people!
  Summer passed, and Shawondasee
Breathed his sighs o'er all the landscape,
From the South-land sent his ardours,
Wafted kisses warm and tender;
And the maize-field grew and ripened,
Till it stood in all the splendour
Of its garments green and yellow,
Of its tassels and its plumage,
And the maize-ears full and shining
Gleamed from bursting sheaths of verdure.
  Then Nokomis, the old woman,
Spake, and said to Minnehaha:
''Tis the Moon when leaves are falling;
All the wild-rice has been gathered,
And the maize is ripe and ready;
Let us gather in the harvest,
Let us wrestle with Mondamin,
Strip him of his plumes and tassels,
Of his garments green and yellow!'
  And the merry Laughing Water
Went rejoicing from the wigwam,
With Nokomis, old and wrinkled,

And they called the women round them,
Called the young men and the maidens,
To the harvest of the cornfields,
To the husking of the maize-ear.

HIAWATHA'S LAMENTATION

In those days the Evil Spirits,
All the Manitos of mischief,
Fearing Hiawatha's wisdom,
And his love for Chibiabos,
Jealous of their faithful friendship,
And their noble words and actions,
Made at length a league against them,
To molest them and destroy them.
  Hiawatha, wise and wary,
Often said to Chibiabos,
'O my brother! do not leave me,
Lest the Evil Spirits harm you!'
Chibiabos, young and heedless,
Laughing shook his coal-black tresses,
Answered ever sweet and childlike,
'Do not fear for me, O brother!
Harm and evil come not near me!'
  Once when Peboan, the Winter,
Roofed with ice the Big-Sea-Water,
When the snow-flakes, whirling downward,
Hissed among the withered oak-leaves,
Changed the pine-trees into wigwams,
Covered all the earth with silence, –
Armed with arrows, shod with snow-shoes,
Heeding not his brother's warning,
Fearing not the Evil Spirits,
Forth to hunt the deer with antlers

All alone went Chibiabos.
  Right across the Big-Sea-Water
Sprang with speed the deer before him.
With the wind and snow he followed,
O'er the treacherous ice he followed,
Wild with all the fierce commotion
And the rapture of the hunting.
  But beneath, the Evil Spirits
Lay in ambush, waiting for him,
Broke the treacherous ice beneath him,
Dragged him downward to the bottom,
Buried in the sand his body.
Unktahee, the god of water,
He the god of the Dacotahs,
Drowned him in the deep abysses
Of the lake of Gitche Gumee.
  From the headlands Hiawatha
Sent forth such a wail of anguish,
Such a fearful lamentation,
That the bison paused to listen,
And the wolves howled from the prairies,
And the thunder in the distance
Starting answered 'Baim-wawa!'
  Then his face with black he painted,
With his robe his head he covered,
In his wigwam sat lamenting,
Seven long weeks he sat lamenting,
Uttering still this moan of sorrow: –
  'He is dead, the sweet musician!
He the sweetest of all singers!
He has gone from us for ever,
He has moved a little nearer
To the Master of all music,

To the Master of all singing!
O my brother, Chibiabos!'
  Then the medicine-men, the Medas,
The magicians, the Wabenos,
And the Jossakeeds, the prophets,
Came to visit Hiawatha;
Built a Sacred Lodge beside him,
To appease him, to console him,
Walked in silent grave procession,
Bearing each a pouch of healing,
Skin of beaver, lynx, or otter,
Filled with magic roots and simples,
Filled with very potent medicines.
  When he heard their steps approaching,
Hiawatha ceased lamenting,
Called no more on Chibiabos;
Naught he questioned, naught he answered,
But his mournful head uncovered,
From his face the mourning colours
Washed he slowly and in silence,
Slowly and in silence followed
Onward to the Sacred Wigwam.
  There a magic drink they gave him,
Made of Nahma-wusk, the spearmint,
And Wabeno-wusk, the yarrow,
Roots of power, and herbs of healing;
Beat their drums, and shook their rattles;
Chanted singly and in chorus,
Mystic songs like these, they chanted.
  'I myself, myself! behold me!
'Tis the great Gray Eagle talking;
Come, ye white crows, come and hear him!
The loud-speaking thunder helps me;

All the unseen spirits help me;
I can hear their voices calling,
All around the sky I hear them!
I can blow you strong, my brother,
I can heal you, Hiawatha!'
'Hi-au-ha!' replied the chorus,
'Way-ha-way!' the mystic chorus.
'Friends of mine are all the serpents!
Hear me shake my skin of hen-hawk!
Mahng, the white loon, I can kill him;
I can shoot your heart and kill it!
I can blow you strong, my brother,
I can heal you, Hiawatha!'
'Hi-au-ha!' replied the chorus,
'Way-ha-way!' the mystic chorus.
'I myself, myself! the prophet!
When I speak the wigwam trembles,
Shakes the Sacred Lodge with terror,
Hands unseen begin to shake it!
When I walk, the sky I tread on
Bends and makes a noise beneath me!
I can blow you strong, my brother!
Rise and speak, O Hiawatha!'
'Hi-au-ha!' replied the chorus,
'Way-ha-way!' the mystic chorus.
Then they shook their medicine-pouches
O'er the head of Hiawatha,
Danced their medicine-dance around him;
And upstarting wild and haggard,
Like a man from dreams awakened,
He was healed of all his madness.
As the clouds are swept from heaven,
Straightway from his brain departed

All his moody melancholy;
As the ice is swept from rivers,
Straightway from his heart departed
All his sorrow and affliction.
Then they summoned Chibiabos
From his grave beneath the waters,
From the sands of Gitche Gumee
Summoned Hiawatha's brother.
And so mighty was the magic
Of that cry and invocation,
That he heard it as he lay there
Underneath the Big-Sea-Water;
From the sand he rose and listened,
Heard the music and the singing,
Came, obedient to the summons,
To the doorway of the wigwam,
But to enter they forbade him.
Through a chink a coal they gave him,
Through the door a burning firebrand;
Ruler in the Land of Spirits,
Ruler o'er the dead, they made him,
Telling him a fire to kindle
For all those that died thereafter,
Camp-fires for their night encampments
On their solitary journey
To the kingdom of Ponemah,
To the land of the Hereafter.
From the village of his childhood,
From the homes of those who knew him,
Passing silent through the forest,
Like a smoke-wreath wafted sideways,
Slowly vanished Chibiabos!
Where he passed, the branches moved not,

Where he trod, the grasses bent not,
And the fallen leaves of last year
Made no sound beneath his footsteps.
  Four whole days he journeyed onward
Down the pathway of the dead men;
On the dead-man's strawberry feasted,
Crossed the melancholy river,
On the swinging log he crossed it,
Came unto the Lake of Silver,
In the Stone Canoe was carried
To the Islands of the Blessed,
To the land of ghosts and shadows.
  On that journey, moving slowly,
Many weary spirits saw he,
Panting under heavy burdens,
Laden with war-clubs, bows and arrows,
Robes of fur, and pots and kettles,
And with food that friends had given
For that solitary journey.
  'Ay! why do the living,' said they,
'Lay such heavy burdens on us!
Better were it to go naked,
Better were it to go fasting,
Than to bear such heavy burdens
On our long and weary journey!'
  Forth then issued Hiawatha,
Wandered eastward, wandered westward,
Teaching men the use of simples
And the antidotes for poisons,
And the cure of all diseases.
Thus was first made known to mortals
All the mystery of Medamin,
All the sacred art of healing.

THE DEATH OF KWASIND

FAR and wide among the nations
Spread the name and fame of Kwasind;
No man dared to strive with Kwasind,
No man could compete with Kwasind.
But the mischievous Puk-Wudjies,
They the envious Little People,
They the fairies and the pigmies,
Plotted and conspired against him.
'If this hateful Kwasind,' said they,
'If this great, outrageous fellow
Goes on thus a little longer,
Tearing everything he touches,
Rending everything to pieces,
Filling all the world with wonder,
What becomes of the Puk-Wudjies?
Who will care for the Puk-Wudjies?
He will tread us down like mushrooms,
Drive us all into the water,
Give our bodies to be eaten
By the wicked Nee-ba-naw-baigs,
By the Spirits of the water!'
So the angry Little People
All conspired against the Strong Man,
All conspired to murder Kwasind,
Yes, to rid the world of Kwasind,
The audacious, overbearing,
Heartless, haughty, dangerous Kwasind!
Now this wondrous strength of Kwasind
In his crown alone was seated;
In his crown too was his weakness;
There alone could he be wounded,

Nowhere else could weapon pierce him,
Nowhere else could weapon harm him.
   Even there the only weapon
That could wound him, that could slay him,
Was the seed-cone of the pine-tree,
Was the blue cone of the fir-tree.
This was Kwasind's fatal secret,
Known to no man among mortals;
But the cunning Little People,
The Puk-Wudjies, knew the secret,
Knew the only way to kill him.
   So they gathered cones together,
Gathered seed-cones of the pine-tree,
Gathered blue cones of the fir-tree,
In the woods by Taquamenaw,
Brought them to the river's margin,
Heaped them in great piles together,
Where the red rocks from the margin
Jutting overhang the river.
There they lay in wait for Kwasind,
The malicious Little People.
   'Twas an afternoon in Summer;
Very hot and still the air was,
Very smooth the gliding river,
Motionless the sleeping shadows:
Insects glistened in the sunshine,
Insects skated on the water,
Filled the drowsy air with buzzing,
With a far-resounding war-cry.
   Down the river came the Strong Man,
In his birch-canoe came Kwasind,
Floating slowly down the current
Of the sluggish Taquamenaw,

Very languid with the weather
Very sleepy with the silence.
  From the overhanging branches,
From the tassels of the birch-trees,
Soft the Spirit of Sleep descended;
By his airy hosts surrounded,
His invisible attendants,
Came the Spirit of Sleep, Nepahwin;
Like the burnished Dush-kwo-neshe,
Like a dragon-fly, he hovered
O'er the drowsy head of Kwasind.
  To his ear there came a murmur
As of waves upon a sea-shore,
As of far-off tumbling waters,
As of winds among the pine-trees;
And he felt upon his forehead
Blows of little airy war-clubs,
Wielded by the slumbrous legions
Of the Spirit of Sleep, Nepahwin,
As of some one breathing on him.
  At the first blow of their war-clubs,
Fell a drowsiness on Kwasind;
At the second blow they smote him,
Motionless his paddle rested;
At the third, before his vision
Reeled the landscape into darkness,
Very sound asleep was Kwasind.
  So he floated down the river,
Like a blind man seated upright,
Floated down the Taquamenaw,
Underneath the trembling birch-trees,
Underneath the wooded headlands,
Underneath the war encampment

Of the pigmies, the Puk-Wudjies.
There they stood, all armed and waiting,
Hurled the pine-cones down upon him,
Struck him on his brawny shoulders,
On his crown defenceless struck him.
'Death to Kwasind!' was the sudden
War-cry of the Little People.
And he sideways swayed and tumbled,
Sideways fell into the river,
Plunged beneath the sluggish water
Headlong, as an otter plunges;
And the birch-canoe, abandoned,
Drifted empty down the river,
Bottom upward swerved and drifted:
Nothing more was seen of Kwasind.
But the memory of the Strong Man
Lingered long among the people,
And whenever through the forest
Raged and roared the wintry tempest,
And the branches, tossed and troubled,
Creaked and groaned and split asunder,
'Kwasind!' cried they; 'that is Kwasind!
He is gathering in his firewood!'

THE GHOSTS

NEVER stoops the soaring vulture
On his quarry in the desert,
On the sick or wounded bison,
But another vulture, watching
From his high aerial look-out,
Sees the downward plunge, and follows;
And a third pursues the second,
Coming from the invisible ether;

First a speck, and then a vulture,
Till the air is dark with pinions.
So disasters come not singly;
But as if they watched and waited,
Scanning one another's motions,
When the first descends, the others
Follow, follow, gathering flockwise
Round their victim, sick and wounded,
First a shadow, then a sorrow,
Till the air is dark with anguish.
Now, o'er all the dreary North-land,
Mighty Peboan, the Winter,
Breathing on the lakes and rivers,
Into stone had changed their waters.
From his hair he shook the snowflakes,
Till the plains were strewn with whiteness,
One uninterrupted level,
As if, stooping, the Creator
With his hand had smoothed them over.
Through the forest, wide and wailing,
Roamed the hunter on his snow-shoes;
In the village worked the women,
Pounded maize, or dressed the deerskin;
And the young men played together
On the ice the noisy ball-play,
On the plain the dance of snow-shoes.
One dark evening, after sundown,
In her wigwam Laughing Water
Sat with old Nokomis, waiting
For the steps of Hiawatha
Homeward from the hunt returning.
On their faces gleamed the firelight,
Painting them with streaks of crimson,

In the eyes of old Nokomis
Glimmered like the watery moonlight,
In the eyes of Laughing Water
Glistened like the sun in water;
And behind them crouched their shadows
In the corners of the wigwam,
And the smoke in wreaths above them
Climbed and crowded through the smoke-flue.
  Then the curtain of the doorway
From without was slowly lifted;
Brighter glowed the fire a moment,
And a moment swerved the smoke-wreath,
As two women entered softly,
Passed the doorway uninvited,
Without word of salutation,
Without sign of recognition,
Sat down in the farthest corner,
Crouching low among the shadows.
  From their aspect and their garments,
Strangers seemed they in the village;
Very pale and haggard were they,
As they sat there sad and silent,
Trembling, cowering with the shadows.
  Was it the wind above the smoke-flue,
Muttering down into the wigwam?
Was it the owl, the Koko-koho,
Hooting from the dismal forest?
Sure a voice said in the silence:
'These are corpses clad in garments,
These are ghosts that come to haunt you,
From the kingdom of Ponemah,
From the land of the Hereafter!'
  Homeward now came Hiawatha

From his hunting in the forest,
With the snow upon his tresses,
And the red deer on his shoulders.
At the feet of Laughing Water
Down he threw his lifeless burden;
Nobler, handsomer she thought him,
Than when first he came to woo her,
First threw down the deer before her,
As a token of his wishes,
As a promise of the future.

Then he turned and saw the strangers,
Cowering, crouching with the shadows;
Said within himself, 'Who are they?
What strange guests has Minnehaha?'
But he questioned not the strangers,
Only spake to bid them welcome
To his lodge, his food, his fireside.

When the evening meal was ready,
And the deer had been divided,
Both the pallid guests, the strangers,
Springing from among the shadows,
Seized upon the choicest portions,
Seized the white fat of the roebuck,
Set apart for Laughing Water,
For the wife of Hiawatha;
Without asking, without thanking,
Eagerly devoured the morsels,
Flitted back among the shadows
In the corner of the wigwam.

Not a word spake Hiawatha,
Not a motion made Nokomis,
Not a gesture Laughing Water;
Not a change came o'er their features;

Only Minnehaha softly
Whispered, saying, 'They are famished;
Let them do what best delights them;
Let them eat, for they are famished.'
  Many a daylight dawned and darkened,
Many a night shook off the daylight
As the pine shakes off the snow-flakes
From the midnight of its branches;
Day by day the guests unmoving
Sat there silent in the wigwam;
But by night, in storm or starlight,
Forth they went into the forest,
Bringing firewood to the wigwam,
Bringing pine-cones for the burning,
Always sad and always silent.
  And whenever Hiawatha
Came from fishing or from hunting,
When the evening meal was ready,
And the food had been divided,
Gliding from their darksome corner,
Came the pallid guests, the strangers,
Seized upon the choicest portions
Set aside for Laughing Water,
And without rebuke or question
Flitted back among the shadows.
  Never once had Hiawatha
By a word or look reproved them;
Never once had old Nokomis
Made a gesture of impatience;
Never once had Laughing Water
Shown resentment at the outrage.
All had they endured in silence,
That the rights of guests and strangers,

That the virtue of free-giving,
By a look might not be lessened,
By a word might not be broken,
Once at midnight Hiawatha,
Ever wakeful, ever watchful,
In the wigwam, dimly lighted
By the brands that still were burning,
By the glimmering, flickering firelight,
Heard a sighing, oft repeated,
Heard a sobbing, as of sorrow.
From his couch rose Hiawatha,
From his shaggy hides of bison,
Pushed aside the deerskin curtain,
Saw the pallid guests, the shadows,
Sitting upright on their couches,
Weeping in the silent midnight.
And he said: 'O guests! why is it
That your hearts are so afflicted,
That you sob so in the midnight?
Has perchance the old Nokomis,
Has my wife, my Minnehaha,
Wronged or grieved you by unkindness,
Failed in hospitable duties?'
Then the shadows ceased from weeping,
Ceased from sobbing and lamenting,
And they said, with gentle voices:
'We are ghosts of the departed,
Souls of those who once were with you.
From the realms of Chibiabos
Hither have we come to try you,
Hither have we come to warn you.
'Cries of grief and lamentation
Reach us in the Blessed Islands;

Cries of anguish from the living,
Calling back their friends departed,
Sadden us with useless sorrow.
Therefore have we come to try you;
No one know us, no one heeds us.
We are but a burden to you,
And we see that the departed
Have no place among the living.
  'Think of this, O Hiawatha!
Speak of it to all the people,
That henceforward and for ever
They no more with lamentations
Sadden the souls of the departed
In the Islands of the Blessed.
  'Do not lay such heavy burdens
In the graves of those you bury,
Not such weight of furs and wampum,
Not such weight of pots and kettles,
For the spirits faint beneath them,
Only give them food to carry,
Only give them fire to light them.
  'Four days is the spirit's journey
To the land of ghosts and shadows,
Four its lonely night encampments;
Four times must their fires be lighted.
Therefore, when the dead are buried,
Let a fire, as night approaches,
Four times on the grave be kindled,
That the soul upon its journey
May not lack the cheerful firelight,
May not grope about in darkness.
  'Farewell, noble Hiawatha!
We have put you to the trial,

To the proof have put your patience,
By the insult of our presence,
By the outrage of our actions.
We have found you great and noble.
Fail not in the greater trial,
Faint not in the harder struggle.'
  When they ceased, a sudden darkness
Fell and filled the silent wigwam.
Hiawatha heard a rustle
As of garments trailing by him,
Heard the curtain of the doorway
Lifted by a hand he saw not,
Felt the cold breath of the night air,
For a moment saw the starlight;
But he saw the ghosts no longer,
Saw no more the wandering spirits
From the kingdom of Ponemah,
From the land of the Hereafter.

THE FAMINE

O THE long and dreary Winter!
O the cold and cruel Winter!
Ever thicker, thicker, thicker
Froze the ice on lake and river,
Ever deeper, deeper, deeper
Fell the snow o'er all the landscape,
Fell the covering snow, and drifted
Through the forest, round the village.
  Hardly from his buried wigwam
Could the hunter force a passage;
With his mittens and his snow-shoes
Vainly walked he through the forest,
Sought for bird or beast and found none,

Saw no track of deer or rabbit,
In the snow beheld no footprints,
In the ghastly, gleaming forest
Fell, and could not rise from weakness,
Perished there from cold and hunger.
  O the famine and the fever!
O the wasting of the famine!
O the blasting of the fever!
O the wailing of the children!
O the anguish of the women!
  All the earth was sick and famished;
Hungry was the air around them,
Hungry was the sky above them,
And the hungry stars in heaven
Like the eyes of wolves glared at them!
  Into Hiawatha's wigwam
Came two other guests, as silent
As the ghosts were, and as gloomy,
Waited not to be invited,
Did not parley at the doorway,
Sat there without word of welcome
In the seat of Laughing Water;
Looked with haggard eyes and hollow
At the face of Laughing Water.
  And the foremost said: 'Behold me!
I am Famine, Bukadawin!'
And the other said: 'Behold me!
I am Fever, Ahkosewin!'
  And the lovely Minnehaha
Shuddered as they looked upon her,
Shuddered at the words they uttered,
Lay down on her bed in silence,
Hid her face, but made no answer;

Lay there trembling, freezing, burning
At the looks they cast upon her,
At the fearful words they uttered.
  Forth into the empty forest
Rushed the maddened Hiawatha;
In his heart was deadly sorrow,
In his face a stony firmness;
On his brow the sweat of anguish
Started, but it froze and fell not.
  Wrapped in furs and armed for hunting,
With his mighty bow of ash-tree,
With his quiver full of arrows,
With his mittens, Minjekahwun,
Into the vast and vacant forest
On his snow-shoes strode he forward.
  'Gitche Manito, the Mighty!'
Cried he with his face uplifted
In that bitter hour of anguish,
'Give your children food, O father!
Give us food, or we must perish!
Give me food for Minnehaha,
For my dying Minnehaha!'
  Through the far-resounding forest,
Through the forest vast and vacant
Rang that cry of desolation,
But there came no other answer
Than the echo of his crying,
Than the echo of the woodlands,
'Minnehaha! Minnehaha!'
  All day long roved Hiawatha
In that melancholy forest,
Through the shadow of whose thickets,
In the pleasant days of Summer,

Of that ne'er forgotten Summer,
He had brought his young wife homeward
From the land of the Dacotahs;
When the birds sang in the thickets,
And the streamlets laughed and glistened,
And the air was full of fragrance,
And the lovely Laughing Water
Said with voice that did not tremble
'I will follow you, my husband!'
  In the wigwam with Nokomis,
With those gloomy guests, that watched her,
With the Famine and the Fever,
She was lying, the Beloved,
She the dying Minnehaha.
  'Hark!' she said; 'I hear a rushing,
Hear a roaring and a rushing,
Hear the Falls of Minnehaha
Calling to me from a distance!'
'No, my child!' said old Nokomis,
''Tis the night-wind in the pine-trees!'
  'Look!' she said; 'I see my father
Standing lonely at his doorway,
Beckoning to me from his wigwam
In the land of the Dacotahs!'
'No, my child!' said old Nokomis,
''Tis the smoke, that waves and beckons!'
'Ah!' said she, 'the eyes of Pauguk
Glare upon me in the darkness,
I can feel his icy fingers
Clasping mine amid the darkness!
Hiawatha! Hiawatha!'
  And the desolate Hiawatha,
Far away amid the forest,

Miles away among the mountains,
Heard that sudden cry of anguish,
Heard the voice of Minnehaha
Calling to him in the darkness,
'Hiawatha! Hiawatha!'
　Over snow-fields waste and pathless,
Under snow-encumbered branches,
Homeward hurried Hiawatha,
Empty-handed, heavy-hearted.
Heard Nokomis moaning, wailing,
'Wahonowin! Wahonowin!
Would that I had perished for you,
Would that I were dead as you are!
Wahonowin! Wahonowin!'
　And he rushed into the wigwam,
Saw the old Nokomis slowly
Rocking to and fro and moaning,
Saw his lovely Minnehaha
Lying dead and cold before him,
And his bursting heart within him
Uttered such a cry of anguish,
That the forest moaned and shuddered,
That the very stars in heaven
Shook and trembled with his anguish.
　Then he sat down still and speechless,
On the bed of Minnehaha,
At the feet of Laughing Water,
At those willing feet, that never
More would lightly run to meet him,
Never more would lightly follow.
　With both hands his face he covered,
Seven long days and nights he sat there,
As if in a swoon he sat there,

Speechless, motionless, unconscious
Of the daylight or the darkness.
  Then they buried Minnehaha;
In the snow a grave they made her,
In the forest deep and darksome,
Underneath the moaning hemlocks;
Clothed her in her richest garments,
Wrapped her in her robes of ermine;
Covered her with snow, like ermine,
Thus they buried Minnehaha.
  And at night a fire was lighted,
On her grave four times was kindled,
For her soul upon its journey
To the Islands of the Blessed.
From his doorway Hiawatha
Saw it burning in the forest,
Lighting up the gloomy hemlocks;
From his sleepless bed uprising,
From the bed of Minnehaha,
Stood and watched it at the doorway,
That it might not be extinguished,
Might not leave her in the darkness.
  'Farewell!' said he, 'Minnehaha!
Farewell, O my Laughing Water!
All my heart is buried with you,
All my thoughts go onward with you!
Come not back again to labour,
Come not back again to suffer,
Where the Famine and the Fever
Wear the heart and waste the body.
Soon my task will be completed,
Soon your footsteps I shall follow
To the Islands of the Blessed,

To the Kingdom of Ponemah,
To the Land of the Hereafter!'

THE WHITE MAN'S FOOT

THUS it was that in the North-land
After that unheard-of coldness,
That intolerable Winter,
Came the Spring with all its splendour,
All its birds and all its blossoms,
All its flowers and leaves and grasses.
Sailing on the wind to northward,
Flying in great flocks, like arrows,
Like huge arrows shot through heaven,
Passed the swan, the Mahnahbezee,
Speaking almost as a man speaks;
And in long lines waving, bending
Like a bowstring snapped asunder,
Came the white goose, Waw-be-wawa;
And in pairs, or singly flying,
Mahng the loon, with clangorous pinions,
The blue heron, the Shuh-shuh-gah,
And the grouse, the Mushkodasa.
In the thickets and the meadows
Piped the bluebird, the Owaissa;
On the summit of the lodges
Sang the robin, the Opechee;
In the covert of the pine-trees
Cooed the pigeon, the Omemee;
And the sorrowing Hiawatha,
Speechless in his infinite sorrow,
Heard their voices calling to him,
Went forth from his gloomy doorway,
Stood and gazed into the heaven,

Gazed upon the earth and waters.
  From his wanderings far to eastward,
From the regions of the morning,
From the shining land of Wabun,
Homeward now returned Iagoo,
The great traveller, the great boaster,
Full of new and strange adventures,
Marvels many and many wonders.
  And the people of the village
Listened to him as he told them
Of his marvellous adventures,
Laughing answered him in this wise:
Ugh! it is indeed Iagoo!
No one else beholds such wonders!
  He had seen, he said, a water
Bigger than the Big-Sea-Water,
Broader than the Gitche Gumee,
Bitter so that none could drink it!
At each other looked the warriors,
Looked the women at each other,
Smiled, and said, 'It cannot be so!
Kaw!' they said, 'it cannot be so!'
  O'er it, said he, o'er this water
Came a great canoe with pinions,
A canoe with wings came flying,
Bigger than a grove of pine-trees,
Taller than the tallest tree-tops!
And the old men and the women
Looked and tittered at each other;
'Kaw!' they said, 'we don't believe it!'
  From its mouth, he said, to greet him,
Came Waywassimo, the lightning,
Came the thunder, Annemeekee!

And the warriors and the women
Laughed aloud at poor Iagoo;
'Kaw!' they said, 'what tales you tell us!'
  In it, said he, came a people,
In a great canoe with pinions
Came, he said, a hundred warriors;
Painted white were all their faces
And with hair their chins were covered!
And the warriors and the women
Laughed and shouted in derision,
Like the ravens on the tree-tops,
Like the crows upon the hemlocks.
'Kaw!' they said, 'what lies you tell us!
Do not think that we believe them!'
  Only Hiawatha laughed not,
But he gravely spake and answered
To their jeering and their jesting:
'True is all Iagoo tells us;
I have seen it in a vision,
Seen the great canoe with pinions,
Seen the people with white faces,
Seen the coming of this bearded
People of the wooden vessel
From the regions of the morning,
From the shining land of Wabun.
  'Gitche Manito, the Mighty,
The Great Spirit, the Creator,
Sends them hither on his errand,
Sends them to us with his message.
Wheresoe'er they move, before them
Swarms the stinging fly, the Ahmo,
Swarms the bee, the honey-maker;
Wheresoe'er they tread, beneath them

Springs a flower unknown among us,
Springs the White-man's foot in blossom.
'Let us welcome, then, the strangers,
Hail them as our friends and brothers,
And the heart's right hand of friendship
Give them when they come to see us.
Gitche Manito, the Mighty,
Said this to me in my vision.
'I beheld, too, in that vision
All the secrets of the future,
Of the distant days that shall be.
I beheld the westward marches
Of the unknown, crowded nations.
All the land was full of people,
Restless, struggling, toiling, striving,
Speaking many tongues, yet feeling
But one heart-beat in their bosoms.
In the woodlands rang their axes,
Smoked their towns in all the valleys,
Over all the lakes and rivers
Rushed their great canoes of thunder.
'Then a darker, drearier vision
Passed before me vague and cloudlike:
I beheld our nation scattered,
All forgetful of my counsels,
Weakened, warring with each other:
Saw the remnants of our people
Sweeping westward, wild and woeful,
Like the cloud-rack of a tempest,
Like the withered leaves of Autumn!'

HIAWATHA'S DEPARTURE

By the shore of Gitche Gumee,
By the shining Big-Sea-Water,
At the doorway of his wigwam,
In the pleasant Summer morning,
Hiawatha stood and waited.
All the air was full of freshness,
All the earth was bright and joyous,
And before him, through the sunshine,
Westward toward the neighbouring forest
Passed in golden swarms the Ahmo,
Passed the bees, the honey-makers,
Burning, singing in the sunshine.
Bright above him shone the heavens,
Level spread the lake before him;
From its bosom leaped the sturgeon,
Sparkling, flashing in the sunshine;
On its margin the great forest
Stood reflected in the water,
Every tree-top had its shadow,
Motionless beneath the water.
From the brow of Hiawatha
Gone was every trace of sorrow,
As the fog from off the water,
As the mist from off the meadow.
With a smile of joy and triumph,
With a look of exultation,
As of one who in a vision
Sees what is to be, but is not,
Stood and waited Hiawatha.
Toward the sun his hands were lifted,
Both the palms spread out against it,
And between the parted fingers

Fell the sunshine on his features,
Flecked with light his naked shoulders,
As it falls and flecks an oak-tree
Through the rifted leaves and branches.
O'er the water floating, flying,
Something in the hazy distance,
Something in the mists of morning,
Loomed and lifted from the water,
Now seemed floating, now seemed flying,
Coming nearer, nearer, nearer.
It was neither goose nor diver,
Neither pelican nor heron,
O'er the water floating, flying,
Through the shining mist of morning,
But a birch-canoe with paddles,
Rising, sinking on the water,
Dripping, flashing in the sunshine;
And within it came a people
From the distant land of Wabun,
From the farthest realms of morning
Came the Black-Robe chief, the Prophet,
He the Priest of Prayer, the Paleface,
With his guides and his companions.
And the noble Hiawatha,
With his hands aloft extended,
Held aloft in sign of welcome,
Waited, full of exultation,
Till the birch-canoe with paddles
Grated on the shining pebbles,
Stranded on the sandy margin,
Till the Black-Robe chief, the Paleface,
With the cross upon his bosom,
Landed on the sandy margin.

Then the joyous Hiawatha
Cried aloud and spake in this wise:
'Beautiful is the sun, O strangers,
When you come so far to see us!
All our town in peace awaits you,
All our doors stand open for you;
You shall enter all our wigwams,
For the heart's right hand we give you.
'Never bloomed the earth so gaily,
Never shone the sun so brightly,
As to-day they shine and blossom
When you come so far to see us!
Never was our lake so tranquil,
Nor so free from rocks and sand-bars;
For your birch-canoe in passing
Has removed both rock and sand-bar.
'Never before had our tobacco
Such a sweet and pleasant flavour,
Never the broad leaves of our cornfields
Were so beautiful to look on,
As they seem to us this morning,
When you come so far to see us!'
And the Black-Robe chief made answer,
Stammered in his speech a little,
Speaking words yet unfamiliar:
'Peace be with you, Hiawatha,
Peace be with you and your people,
Peace of prayer, and peace of pardon,
Peace of Christ, and joy of Mary!'
Then the generous Hiawatha
Led the strangers to his wigwam,
Seated them on skins of bison,
Seated them on skins of ermine,

And the careful, old Nokomis
Brought them food in bowls of bass-wood,
Water brought in birchen dippers,
And the calumet, the peace-pipe,
Filled and lighted for their smoking.
  All the old men of the village,
All the warriors of the nation,
All the Jossakeeds, the prophets,
The magicians, the Wabenos,
And the medicine-men, the Medas,
Came to bid the strangers welcome;
'It is well,' they said, 'O brothers,
That you come so far to see us!'
  In a circle round the doorway,
With their pipes they sat in silence,
Waiting to behold the strangers,
Waiting to receive their message;
Till the Black-Robe chief, the Paleface,
From the wigwam came to greet them,
Stammering in his speech a little,
Speaking words yet unfamiliar;
'It is well,' they said, 'O brother,
That you come so far to see us!'
  Then the Black-Robe chief, the prophet,
Told his message to the people,
Told the purport of his mission,
Told them of the Virgin Mary,
And her blessed Son, the Saviour,
How in distant lands and ages
He had lived on earth as we do;
How he fasted, prayed, and laboured;
How the Jews, the tribe accursed,
Mocked him, scourged him, crucified him;

How he rose from where they laid him,
Walked again with his disciples,
And ascended into heaven.
  And the chiefs made answer, saying:
'We have listened to your message,
We have heard your words of wisdom,
We will think on what you tell us.
It is well for us, O brothers,
That you come so far to see us!'
  Then they rose up and departed
Each one homeward to his wigwam,
To the young men and the women,
Told the story of the strangers
Whom the Master of Life had sent them
From the shining land of Wabun.
  Heavy with the heat and silence
Grew the afternoon of Summer;
With a drowsy sound the forest
Whispered round the sultry wigwam,
With a sound of sleep the water
Rippled on the beach below it;
From the cornfields shrill and ceaseless
Sang the grasshopper, Pah-puk-keena;
And the guests of Hiawatha,
Weary with the heat of Summer,
Slumbered in the sultry wigwam.
  Slowly o'er the simmering landscape
Fell the evening's dusk and coolness,
And the long and level sunbeams
Shot their spears into the forest,
Breaking through its shields of shadow,
Rushed into each secret ambush,
Searched each thicket, dingle, hollow;

Still the guests of Hiawatha
Slumbered in the silent wigwam.
From his place rose Hiawatha,
Bade farewell to old Nokomis,
Spake in whispers, spake in this wise,
Did not wake the guests, that slumbered:
'I am going, O Nokomis,
On a long and distant journey,
To the portals of the Sunset,
To the regions of the home-wind,
Of the Northwest-Wind, Keewaydin.
But these guests I leave behind me,
In your watch and ward I leave them;
See that never harm comes near them,
See that never fear molests them,
Never danger nor suspicion,
Never want of food or shelter,
In the lodge of Hiawatha!'
Forth into the village went he,
Bade farewell to all the warriors,
Bade farewell to all the young men,
Spake persuading, spake in this wise:
'I am going, O my people,
On a long and distant journey;
Many moons and many winters
Will have come, and will have vanished,
Ere I come again to see you.
But my guests I leave behind me;
Listen to their words of wisdom,
Listen to the truth they tell you,
For the Master of Life has sent them
From the land of light and morning!'

On the shore stood Hiawatha,
Turned and waved his hand at parting;
On the clear and luminous water
Launched his birch-canoe for sailing,
From the pebbles of the margin
Shoved it forth into the water;
Whispered to it, 'Westward! westward!'
And with speed it darted forward.
And the evening sun descending
Set the clouds on fire with redness,
Burned the broad sky like a prairie,
Left upon the level water
One long track and trail of splendour,
Down whose stream, as down a river,
Westward, westward Hiawatha
Sailed into the fiery sunset,
Sailed into the purple vapours,
Sailed into the dusk of evening.
And the people from the margin
Watched him floating, rising, sinking,
Till the birch-canoe seemed lifted
High into that sea of splendour,
Till it sank into the vapours
Like the new moon slowly, slowly
Sinking in the purple distance.
And they said, 'Farewell for ever!'
Said, 'Farewell, O Hiawatha!'
And the forests, dark and lonely,
Moved through all their depths of darkness,
Sighed, 'Farewell, O Hiawatha!'
And the waves upon the margin
Rising, rippling on the pebbles,
Sobbed, 'Farewell, O Hiawatha!'

And the heron, the Shuh-shuh-gah,
From her haunts among the fenlands,
Screamed, 'Farewell, O Hiawatha!'
  Thus departed Hiawatha,
Hiawatha the Beloved,
In the glory of the sunset,
In the purple mists of evening,
To the regions of the home-wind,
Of the Northwest-Wind Keewaydin,
To the Islands of the Blessed,
To the kingdom of Ponemah,
To the land of the Hereafter!

Paul Revere's Ride

Henry Wadsworth Longfellow

First published in the magazine *Atlantic Monthly*, January 1861, about an event in 1775

LISTEN, my children, and you shall hear
Of the midnight ride of Paul Revere,
On the eighteenth of April, in Seventy-five;
Hardly a man is now alive
Who remembers that famous day and year.

He said to his friend, 'If the British march
By land or sea from the town tonight,
Hang a lantern aloft in the belfry arch
Of the North Church tower as a signal light –
One, if by land, and two, if by sea;
And I on the opposite shore will be,
Ready to ride and spread the alarm
Through every Middlesex village and farm,
For the country folk to be up and to arm.'

Then he said 'Good night!' and with muffled oar
Silently rowed to the Charlestown shore,
Just as the moon rose over the bay,
Where swinging wide at her moorings lay
The *Somerset*, British man-of-war;
A phantom ship, with each mast and spar
Across the moon like a prison bar,

And a huge black hulk, that was magnified
By its own reflection in the tide.
Meanwhile, his friend, through alley and street,
Wanders and watches with eager ears,
Till in the silence around him he hears
The muster of men at the barrack door,
The sound of arms, and the tramp of feet,
And the measured tread of the grenadiers
Marching down to their boats on the shore.

Then he climbed the tower of the Old North Church,
By the wooden stairs, with stealthy tread,
To the belfry chamber overhead,
And startled the pigeons from their perch
On the sombre rafters, that round him made
Masses and moving shapes of shade –
By the trembling ladder, steep and tall,
To the highest window in the wall,
Where he paused to listen and look down
A moment on the roofs of the town,
And the moonlight flowing over all.

Beneath, in the churchyard, lay the dead,
In their night-encampment on the hill,
Wrapped in silence so deep and still
That he could hear, like a sentinel's tread,
The watchful night-wind, as it went
Creeping along from tent to tent,
And seeming to whisper, 'All is well!'
A moment only he feels the spell
Of the place and the hour, and the secret dread
Of the lonely belfry and the dead;
For suddenly all his thoughts are bent

On a shadowy something far away,
Where the river widens to meet the bay –
A line of black that bends and floats
On the rising tide, like a bridge of boats.

Meanwhile, impatient to mount and ride,
Booted and spurred, with a heavy stride
On the opposite shore walked Paul Revere.
Now he patted his horse's side,
Now gazed at the landscape far and near,
Then, impetuous, stamped the earth,
And turned and tightened his saddle-girth;
But mostly he watched with eager search
The belfry-tower of the Old North Church,
As it rose above the graves on the hill,
Lonely and spectral and sombre and still.
And lo! as he looks, on the belfry's height
A glimmer, and then a gleam of light!
He springs to the saddle, the bridle he turns,
But lingers and gazes, till full on his sight
A second lamp in the belfry burns!

A hurry of hoofs in a village street,
A shape in the moonlight, a bulk in the dark,
And beneath, from the pebbles, in passing, a spark
Struck out by a steed flying fearless and fleet:
That was all! And yet, through the gloom and the light,
The fate of a nation was riding that night;
And the spark struck out by that steed, in his flight,
Kindled the land into flame with its heat.

He has left the village and mounted the steep,
And beneath him, tranquil and broad and deep,

Is the Mystic, meeting the ocean tides;
And under the alders, that skirt its edge,
Now soft on the sand, now loud on the ledge,
Is heard the tramp of his steed as he rides.

It was twelve by the village clock
When he crossed the bridge into Medford town.
He heard the crowing of the cock,
And the barking of the farmer's dog,
And felt the damp of the river fog,
That rises after the sun goes down.

It was one by the village clock,
When he galloped into Lexington.
He saw the gilded weathercock
Swim in the moonlight as he passed,
And the meeting-house windows, blank and bare,
Gaze at him with a spectral glare,
As if they already stood aghast
At the bloody work they would look upon.

It was two by the village clock,
When he came to the bridge in Concord town.
He heard the bleating of the flock,
And the twitter of birds among the trees,
And felt the breath of the morning breeze
Blowing over the meadows brown.
And one was safe and asleep in his bed
Who at the bridge would be first to fall,
Who that day would be lying dead,
Pierced by a British musket-ball.

You know the rest. In the books you have read,
How the British Regulars fired and fled,
How the farmers gave them ball for ball,
From behind each fence and farmyard wall;
Chasing the red-coats down the lane,
Then crossing the fields to emerge again
Under the trees at the turn of the road,
And only pausing to fire and load.

So through the night rode Paul Revere;
And so through the night went his cry of alarm
To every Middlesex village and farm –
A cry of defiance and not of fear,
A voice in the darkness, a knock at the door,
And a word that shall echo for evermore!
For, borne on a night-wind of the Past,
Through all our history, to the last,
In the hour of darkness and peril and need,
The people will waken and listen to hear
The hurrying hoof-beats of that steed,
And the midnight message of Paul Revere.

Sohrab and Rustum

Matthew Arnold

This version first published in *Poems* (1885)

And the first grey of morning filled the east,
And the fog rose out of the Oxus stream.
But all the Tartar camp along the stream
Was hushed, and still the men were plunged in sleep:
Sohrab alone, he slept not: all night long
He had lain wakeful, tossing on his bed;
But when the grey dawn stole into his tent,
He rose, and clad himself, and girt his sword,
And took his horseman's cloak, and left his tent,
And went abroad into the cold wet fog,
Through the dim camp to Peran-Wisa's tent.
Through the black Tartar tents he passed, which stood
Clustering like bee-hives on the low flat strand
Of Oxus, where the summer floods o'erflow
When the sun melts the snows in high Pamere:
Through the black tents he passed, o'er that low strand,
And to a hillock came, a little back
From the stream's brink, the spot where first a boat,
Crossing the stream in summer, scrapes the land.
The men of former times had crowned the top
With a clay fort: but that was fallen; and now
The Tartars built there Peran-Wisa's tent,
A dome of laths, and o'er it felts were spread.
And Sohrab came there, and went in, and stood
Upon the thick-piled carpets in the tent,

And found the old man sleeping on his bed
Of rugs and felts, and near him lay his arms.
And Peran-Wisa heard him, though the step
Was dulled; for he slept light, an old man's sleep;
And he rose quickly on one arm, and said:
  'Who art thou? for it is not yet clear dawn.
Speak! is there news, or any night alarm?'
  But Sohrab came to the bedside, and said:
'Thou know'st me, Peran-Wisa: it is I.
The sun is not yet risen, and the foe
Sleep; but I sleep not; all night long I lie
Tossing and wakeful, and I come to thee.
For so did King Afrasiab bid me seek
Thy counsel, and to heed thee as thy son,
In Samarcand, before the army marched;
And I will tell thee what my heart desires.
Thou know'st if, since from Ader-baijan first
I came among the Tartars, and bore arms,
I have still served Afrasiab well, and shown,
At my boy's years, the courage of a man.
This too thou know'st, that, while I still bear on
The conquering Tartar ensigns through the world,
And beat the Persians back on every field,
I seek one man, one man, and one alone –
Rustum, my father; who, I hoped, should greet,
Should one day greet, upon some well-fought field
His not unworthy, not inglorious son.
So I long hoped, but him I never find.
Come then, hear now, and grant me what I ask.
Let the two armies rest today: but I
Will challenge forth the bravest Persian lords
To meet me, man to man: if I prevail,
Rustum will surely hear it; if I fall –

Old man, the dead need no one, claim no kin.
Dim is the rumour of a common fight,
Where host meets host, and many names are sunk:
But of a single combat fame speaks clear.'
He spoke: and Peran-Wisa took the hand
Of the young man in his, and sighed, and said:
'O Sohrab, an unquiet heart is thine!
Canst thou not rest among the Tartar chiefs,
And share the battle's common chance with us
Who love thee, but must press for ever first,
In single fight incurring single risk,
To find a father thou hast never seen?
That were far best, my son, to stay with us
Unmurmuring; in our tents, while it is war,
And when 'tis truce, then in Afrasiab's towns.
But, if this one desire indeed rules all,
To seek out Rustum – seek him not through fight:
Seek him in peace, and carry to his arms,
O Sohrab, carry an unwounded son!
But far hence seek him, for he is not here.
For now it is not as when I was young,
When Rustum was in front of every fray:
But now he keeps apart, and sits at home,
In Seistan, with Zal, his father old.
Whether that his own mighty strength at last
Feels the abhorred approaches of old age;
Or in some quarrel with the Persian King.
There go! – Thou wilt not? Yet my heart forbodes
Danger or death awaits thee on this field.
Fain would I know thee safe and well, though lost
To us: fain therefore send thee hence, in peace
To seek thy father, not seek single fights
In vain: – but who can keep the lion's cub

From ravening? and who govern Rustum's son?
Go: I will grant thee what thy heart desires.'
So said he, and dropped Sohrab's hand, and left
His bed, and the warm rugs whereon he lay,
And o'er his chilly limbs his woollen coat
He passed, and tied his sandals on his feet,
And threw a white cloak round him, and he took
In his right hand a ruler's staff, no sword;
And on his head he set his sheepskin cap,
Black, glossy, curled, the fleece of Kara-Kul;
And raised the curtain of his tent, and called
His herald to his side, and went abroad.
The sun, by this, had risen, and cleared the fog
From the broad Oxus and the glittering sands:
And from their tents the Tartar horsemen filed
Into the open plain; so Haman bade;
Haman, who next to Peran-Wisa ruled
The host, and still was in his lusty prime.
From their black tents, long files of horse, they streamed:
As when, some grey November morn, the files,
In marching order spread, of long-necked cranes,
Stream over Casbin, and the southern slopes
Of Elburz, from the Aralian estuaries.
Or some frore Caspian reed-bed, southward bound
For the warm Persian sea-board: so they streamed.
The Tartars of the Oxus, the King's guard,
First, with black sheepskin caps and with long spears;
Large men, large steeds; who from Bokhara come
And Khiva, and ferment the milk of mares.
Next the more temperate Toorkmuns of the south,
The Tukas, and the lances of Salore,
And those from Attruck and the Caspian sands;
Light men, and on light steeds, who only drink

The acrid milk of camels, and their wells.
And then a swarm of wandering horse, who came
From far, and a more doubtful service owned;
The Tartars of Ferghana, from the banks
Of the Jaxartes, men with scanty beards
And close-set skull-caps; and those wilder hordes
Who roam o'er Kipchak and the northern waste,
Kalmuks and unkemped Kuzzaks, tribes who stray
Nearest the Pole, and wandering Kirghizzes,
Who come on shaggy ponies from Pamere.
These all filed out from camp into the plain.
And on the other side the Persians formed:
First a light cloud of horse, Tartars they seemed,
The Ilyats of Khorassan: and behind,
The royal troops of Persia, horse and foot,
Marshalled battalions bright in burnished steel.
But Peran-Wisa with his herald came
Threading the Tartar squadrons to the front,
And with his staff kept back the foremost ranks.
And when Ferood, who led the Persians, saw
That Peran-Wisa kept the Tartars back,
He took his spear, and to the front he came,
And checked his ranks, and fixed them where they stood.
And the old Tartar came upon the sand
Betwixt the silent hosts, and spake, and said:
'Ferood, and ye, Persians and Tartars, hear!
Let there be truce between the hosts today.
But choose a champion from the Persian lords
To fight our champion Sohrab, man to man.'
As, in the country, on a morn in June,
When the dew glistens on the pearled ears,
A shiver runs through the deep corn for joy –
So, when they heard what Peran-Wisa said,

A thrill through all the Tartar squadrons ran
Of pride and hope for Sohrab, whom they loved.
  But as a troop of pedlars, from Cabool,
Cross underneath the Indian Caucasus,
That vast sky-neighbouring mountain of milk snow;
Winding so high, that, as they mount, they pass
Long flocks of travelling birds dead on the snow,
Choked by the air, and scarce can they themselves
Slake their parched throats with sugared mulberries –
In single file they move, and stop their breath,
For fear they should dislodge the o'erhanging snows –
So the pale Persians held their breath with fear.
  And to Ferood his brother chiefs came up
To counsel: Gudurz and Zoarrah came,
And Feraburz, who ruled the Persian host
Second, and was the uncle of the King:
These came and counselled; and then Gudurz said:
  'Ferood, shame bids us take their challenge up,
Yet champion have we none to match this youth.
He has the wild stag's foot, the lion's heart.
But Rustum came last night; aloof he sits
And sullen, and has pitched his tents apart:
Him will I seek, and carry to his ear
The Tartar challenge, and this young man's name.
Haply he will forget his wrath, and fight.
Stand forth the while, and take their challenge up.'
  So spake he; and Ferood stood forth and said:
'Old man, be it agreed as thou hast said.
Let Sohrab arm, and we will find a man.'
  He spoke; and Peran-Wisa turned, and strode
Back through the opening squadrons to his tent.
But through the anxious Persians Gudurz ran,
And crossed the camp which lay behind, and reached,

Out on the sands beyond it, Rustum's tents.
Of scarlet cloth they were, and glittering gay,
Just pitched: the high pavilion in the midst
Was Rustum's, and his men lay camped around.
And Gudurz entered Rustum's tent, and found
Rustum: his morning meal was done, but still
The table stood before him, charged with food –
A side of roasted sheep, and cakes of bread,
And dark green melons; and there Rustum sate
Listless, and held a falcon on his wrist,
And played with it; but Gudurz came and stood
Before him; and he looked, and saw him stand;
And with a cry sprang up, and dropped the bird,
And greeted Gudurz with both hands, and said:
'Welcome! these eyes could see no better sight.
What news? but sit down first, and eat and drink.'
But Gudurz stood in the tent door, and said:
'Not now: a time will come to eat and drink,
But not today: today has other needs.
The armies are drawn out, and stand at gaze:
For from the Tartars is a challenge brought
To pick a champion from the Persian lords
To fight their champion – and thou know'st his name –
Sohrab men call him, but his birth is hid.
O Rustum, like thy might is this young man's!
He has the wild stag's foot, the lion's heart.
And he is young, and Iran's chiefs are old,
Or else too weak; and all eyes turn to thee.
Come down and help us, Rustum, or we lose.'
He spoke: but Rustum answered with a smile:
'Go to! if Iran's chiefs are old, then I
Am older: if the young are weak, the King
Errs strangely: for the King, for Kai Khosroo,

Himself is young, and honours younger men,
And lets the aged moulder to their graves.
Rustum he loves no more, but loves the young –
The young may rise at Sohrab's vaunts, not I.
For what care I, though all speak Sohrab's fame?
For would that I myself had such a son,
And not that one slight helpless girl I have,
A son so famed, so brave, to send to war.
And I to tarry with the snow-haired Zal,
My father, whom the robber Afghans vex,
And clip his borders short, and drive his herds,
And he has none to guard his weak old age.
There would I go, and hang my armour up,
And with my great name fence that weak old man,
And spend the goodly treasures I have got,
And rest my age, and hear of Sohrab's fame,
And leave to death the hosts of thankless kings,
And with these slaughterous hands draw sword no more.'
He spoke, and smiled; and Gudurz made reply:
'What then, O Rustum, will men say to this,
When Sohrab dares our bravest forth, and seeks
Thee most of all, and thou, whom most he seeks,
Hidest thy face? Take heed, lest men should say,
Like some old miser, Rustum hoards his fame,
And shuns to peril it with younger men.'
And greatly moved, then Rustum made reply:
'O Gudurz, wherefore dost thou say such words?
Thou knowest better words than this to say.
What is one more, or less, obscure or famed,
Valiant or craven, young or old, to me?
Are not they mortal, am not I myself?
But who for men of naught would do great deeds?
Come, thou shalt see how Rustum hoards his fame.

But I will fight unknown, and in plain arms;
Let not men say of Rustum, he was matched
In single fight with any mortal man.'
He spoke, and frowned; and Gudurz turned, and ran
Back quickly through the camp in fear and joy,
Fear at his wrath, but joy that Rustum came.
But Rustum strode to his tent door, and called
His followers in, and bade them bring his arms,
And clad himself in steel: the arms he chose
Were plain, and on his shield was no device,
Only his helm was rich, inlaid with gold,
And from the fluted spine atop a plume
Of horsehair waved, a scarlet horsehair plume.
So armed he issued forth; and Ruksh, his horse,
Followed him, like a faithful hound, at heel –
Ruksh, whose renown was noised through all the earth,
The horse, whom Rustum on a foray once
Did in Bokhara by the river find
A colt beneath its dam, and drove him home,
And reared him; a bright bay, with lofty crest;
Dight with a saddle-cloth of broidered green
Crusted with gold, and on the ground were worked
All beasts of chase, all beasts which hunters know:
So followed, Rustum left his tents, and crossed
The camp, and to the Persian host appeared.
And all the Persians knew him, and with shouts
Hailed; but the Tartars knew not who he was.
And dear as the wet diver to the eyes
Of his pale wife who waits and weeps on shore,
By sandy Bahrein, in the Persian Gulf,
Plunging all day in the blue waves, at night,
Having made up his tale of precious pearls,
Rejoins her in their hut upon the sands –

So dear to the pale Persians Rustum came.
  And Rustum to the Persian front advanced,
And Sohrab armed in Haman's tent, and came.
And as afield the reapers cut a swathe
Down through the middle of a rich man's corn,
And on each side are squares of standing corn,
And in the midst a stubble, short and bare;
So on each side were squares of men, with spears
Bristling, and in the midst, the open sand.
And Rustum came upon the sand, and cast
His eyes towards the Tartar tents, and saw
Sohrab come forth, and eyed him as he came.
  As some rich woman, on a winter's morn,
Eyes through her silken curtains the poor drudge
Who with numb blackened fingers makes her fire –
At cock-crow, on a starlit winter's morn,
When the frost flowers the whitened window panes –
And wonders how she lives, and what the thoughts
Of that poor drudge may be; so Rustum eyed
The unknown adventurous youth, who from afar
Came seeking Rustum, and defying forth
All the most valiant chiefs: long he perused
His spirited air, and wondered who he was.
For very young he seemed, tenderly reared;
Like some young cypress, tall, and dark, and straight,
Which in a queen's secluded garden throws
Its slight dark shadow on the moonlit turf,
By midnight, to a bubbling fountain's sound –
So slender Sohrab seemed, so softly reared.
And a deep pity entered Rustum's soul
As he beheld him coming; and he stood,
And beckoned to him with his hand, and said:
  'O thou young man, the air of Heaven is soft,

And warm, and pleasant; but the grave is cold.
Heaven's air is better than the cold dead grave.
Behold me: I am vast, and clad in iron,
And tried; and I have stood on many a field
Of blood, and I have fought with many a foe:
Never was that field lost, or that foe saved.
O Sohrab, wherefore wilt thou rush on death?
Be governed: quit the Tartar host, and come
To Iran, and be as my son to me,
And fight beneath my banner till I die.
There are no youths in Iran brave as thou.'

So he spake, mildly: Sohrab heard his voice,
The mighty voice of Rustum; and he saw
His giant figure planted on the sand,
Sole, like some single tower, which a chief
Has builded on the waste in former years
Against the robbers; and he saw that head,
Streaked with its first grey hairs: hope filled his soul;
And he ran forwards and embraced his knees,
And clasped his hand within his own and said:

'Oh, by thy father's head! by thine own soul!
Art thou not Rustum? Speak! art thou not he?'

But Rustum eyed askance the kneeling youth,
And turned away, and spoke to his own soul:

'Ah me, I muse what this young fox may mean.
False, wily, boastful, are these Tartar boys.
For if I now confess this thing he asks,
And hide it not, but say – *Rustum is here* –
He will not yield indeed, nor quit our foes,
But he will find some pretext not to fight,
And praise my fame, and proffer courteous gifts,
A belt or sword perhaps, and go his way.
And on a feast-tide, in Afrasiab's hall,

In Samarcand, he will arise and cry –
"I challenged once, when the two armies camped
Beside the Oxus, all the Persian lords
To cope with me in single fight; but they
Shrank; only Rustum dared: then he and I
Changed gifts, and went on equal terms away."
So will he speak, perhaps, while men applaud.
Then were the chiefs of Iran shamed through me.'
   And then he turned, and sternly spake aloud:
'Rise! wherefore dost thou vainly question thus
Of Rustum? I am here, whom thou hast called
By challenge forth: make good thy vaunt, or yield.
Is it with Rustum only thou wouldst fight?
Rash boy, men look on Rustum's face and flee.
For well I know, that did great Rustum stand
Before thy face this day, and were revealed,
There would be then no talk of fighting more.
But being what I am, I tell thee this;
Do thou record it in thine inmost soul:
Either thou shalt renounce thy vaunt, and yield;
Or else thy bones shall strew this sand, till winds
Bleach them, or Oxus with his summer floods,
Oxus in summer wash them all away.'
   He spoke: and Sohrab answered, on his feet:
'Art thou so fierce? Thou wilt not fright me so.
I am no girl, to be made pale by words.
Yet this thou hast said well, did Rustum stand
Here on this field, there were no fighting then.
But Rustum is far hence, and we stand here.
Begin: thou art more vast, more dread than I,
And thou art proved, I know, and I am young –
But yet success sways with the breath of Heaven.
And though thou thinkest that thou knowest sure

Thy victory, yet thou canst not surely know.
For we are all, like swimmers in the sea,
Poised on the top of a huge wave of fate,
Which hangs uncertain to which side to fall.
And whether it will heave us up to land,
Or whether it will roll us out to sea,
Back out to sea, to the deep waves of death,
We know not, and no search will make us know:
Only the event will teach us in its hour.'
  He spoke; and Rustum answered not, but hurled
His spear: down from the shoulder, down it came,
As on some partridge in the corn a hawk
That long has towered in the airy clouds
Drops like a plummet: Sohrab saw it come,
And sprang aside, quick as a flash: the spear
Hissed, and went quivering down into the sand,
Which it sent flying wide: then Sohrab threw
In turn, and full struck Rustum's shield: sharp rang,
The iron plates rang sharp, but turned the spear.
And Rustum seized his club, which none but he
Could wield: an unlopped trunk it was, and huge,
Still rough; like those which men in treeless plains
To build them boats fish from the flooded rivers,
Hyphasis or Hydaspes, when, high up
By their dark springs, the wind in winter time
Has made in Himalayan forests wrack,
And strewn the channels with torn boughs; so huge
The club which Rustum lifted now, and struck
One stroke; but again Sohrab sprang aside
Lithe as the glancing snake, and the club came
Thundering to earth, and leapt from Rustum's hand.
And Rustum followed his own blow, and fell
To his knees, and with his fingers clutched the sand:

And now might Sohrab have unsheathed his sword,
And pierced the mighty Rustum while he lay
Dizzy, and on his knees, and choked with sand:
But he looked on, and smiled, nor bared his sword,
But courteously drew back, and spoke, and said:
'Thou strik'st too hard: that club of thine will float
Upon the summer floods, and not my bones.
But rise, and be not wroth; not wroth am I:
No, when I see thee, wrath forsakes my soul.
Thou say'st, thou art not Rustum: be it so.
Who art thou then, that canst so touch my soul?
Boy as I am, I have seen battles too;
Have waded foremost in their bloody waves,
And heard their hollow roar of dying men;
But never was my heart thus touched before.
Are they from Heaven, these softenings of the heart?
O thou old warrior, let us yield to Heaven!
Come, plant we here in earth our angry spears,
And make a truce, and sit upon this sand,
And pledge each other in red wine, like friends,
And thou shalt talk to me of Rustum's deeds.
There are enough foes in the Persian host
Whom I may meet, and strike, and feel no pang;
Champions enough Afrasiab has, whom thou
Mayst fight; fight them, when they confront thy spear.
But oh, let there be peace 'twixt thee and me!'
He ceased: but while he spake, Rustum had risen,
And stood erect, trembling with rage: his club
He left to lie, but had regained his spear,
Whose fiery point now in his mailed right hand
Blazed bright and baleful, like that autumn star,
The baleful sign of fevers: dust had soiled
His stately crest, and dimmed his glittering arms.

His breast heaved; his lips foamed; and twice his voice
Was choked with rage: at last these words broke way:
'Girl! nimble with thy feet, not with thy hands!
Curled minion, dancer, coiner of sweet words!
Fight; let me hear thy hateful voice no more!
Thou art not in Afrasiab's gardens now
With Tartar girls, with whom thou art wont to dance;
But on the Oxus sands, and in the dance
Of battle, and with me, who make no play
Of war: I fight it out, and hand to hand.
Speak not to me of truce, and pledge, and wine!
Remember all thy valour: try thy feints
And cunning: all the pity I had is gone:
Because thou has shamed me before both the hosts
With thy light skipping tricks, and thy girl's wiles.'
He spoke; and Sohrab kindled at his taunts.
And he too drew his sword: at once they rushed
Together, as two eagles on one prey
Come rushing down together from the clouds,
One from the east, one from the west: their shields
Dashed with a clang together, and a din
Rose, such as that the sinewy woodcutters
Make often in the forest's heart at morn,
Of hewing axes, crashing trees: such blows
Rustum and Sohrab on each other hailed.
And you would say that sun and stars took part
In that unnatural conflict; for a cloud
Grew suddenly in Heaven, and darked the sun
Over the fighters' heads; and a wind rose
Under their feet, and moaning swept the plain,
And in a sandy whirlwind wrapped the pair.
In gloom they twain were wrapped, and they alone;
For both the on-looking hosts on either hand

Stood in broad daylight, and the sky was pure,
And the sun sparkled on the Oxus stream.
But in the gloom they fought, with bloodshot eyes
And labouring breath; first Rustum struck the shield
Which Sohrab held stiff out: the steel-spiked spear
Rent the tough plates, but failed to reach the skin,
And Rustum plucked it back with angry groan.
Then Sohrab with his sword smote Rustum's helm,
Nor clove its steel quite through; but all the crest
He shore away, and that proud horsehair plume,
Never till now defiled, sunk to the dust;
And Rustum bowed his head; but then the gloom
Grew blacker: thunder rumbled in the air,
And lightnings rent the cloud; and Ruksh, the horse,
Who stood at hand, uttered a dreadful cry:
No horse's cry was that, most like the roar
Of some pained desert lion, who all day
Has trailed the hunter's javelin in his side,
And comes at night to die upon the sand:
The two hosts heard that cry, and quaked for fear,
And Oxus curdled as it crossed his stream.
But Sohrab heard, and quailed not, but rushed on,
And struck again; and again Rustum bowed
His head; but this time all the blade, like glass,
Sprang in a thousand shivers on the helm,
And in his hand the hilt remained alone.
Then Rustum raised his head: his dreadful eyes
Glared, and he shook on high his menacing spear,
And shouted, *Rustum!* Sohrab heard that shout,
And shrank amazed: back he recoiled one step,
And scanned with blinking eyes the advancing form:
And then he stood bewildered; and he dropped
His covering shield, and the spear pierced his side.

He reeled, and staggering back, sunk to the ground.
And then the gloom dispersed, and the wind fell,
And the bright sun broke forth, and melted all
The cloud; and the two armies saw the pair;
Saw Rustum standing, safe upon his feet,
And Sohrab, wounded on the bloody sand.
  Then, with a bitter smile, Rustum began:
'Sohrab, thou thoughtest in thy mind to kill
A Persian lord this day, and strip his corpse,
And bear thy trophies to Afrasiab's tent.
Or else that the great Rustum would come down
Himself to fight, and that thy wiles would move
His heart to take a gift, and let thee go.
And then that all the Tartar host would praise
Thy courage or thy craft, and spread thy fame,
To glad thy father in his weak old age.
Fool! thou art slain, and by an unknown man!
Dearer to the red jackals shalt thou be,
Than to thy friends, and to thy father old.'
  And with a fearless mien Sohrab replied:
'Unknown thou art; yet thy fierce vaunt is vain.
Thou dost not slay me, proud and boastful man!
No! Rustum slays me, and this filial heart.
For were I matched with ten such men as thee,
And I were he who till today I was,
They should be lying here, I standing there.
But that beloved name unnerved my arm –
That name, and something, I confess, in thee,
Which troubles all my heart, and made my shield
Fall; and thy spear transfixed an unarmed foe.
And now thou boastest, and insult'st my fate.
But hear thou this, fierce man, tremble to hear!
The mighty Rustum shall avenge my death!

My father, whom I seek through all the world,
He shall avenge my death, and punish thee!'
  As when some hunter in the spring hath found
A breeding eagle sitting on her nest,
Upon the craggy isle of a hill lake,
And pierced her with an arrow as she rose,
And followed her to find out where she fell
Far off; – anon her mate comes winging back
From hunting, and a great way off descries
His huddling young left sole; at that, he checks
His pinion, and with short uneasy sweeps
Circles above his eyrie, with loud screams
Chiding his mate back to her nest; but she
Lies dying, with the arrow in her side,
In some far stony gorge out of his ken,
A heap of fluttering feathers: never more
Shall the lake glass her, flying over it;
Never the black and dripping precipices
Echo her stormy scream as she sails by: –
As that poor bird flies home, nor knows his loss –
So Rustum knew not his own loss, but stood
Over his dying son, and knew him not.
  But with a cold, incredulous voice, he said:
'What prate is this of fathers and revenge?
The mighty Rustum never had a son.'
  And, with a failing voice, Sohrab replied:
'Ah yes, he had! and that lost son am I.
Surely the news will one day reach his ear,
Reach Rustum, where he sits, and tarries long,
Somewhere, I know not where, but far from here;
And pierce him like a stab, and make him leap
To arms, and cry for vengeance upon thee.
Fierce man, bethink thee, for an only son

What will that grief, what will that vengeance be!
Oh, could I live, till I that grief had seen!
Yet him I pity not so much, but her,
My mother, who in Ader-baijan dwells
With that old King, her father, who grows grey
With age, and rules over the valiant Koords.
Her most I pity, who no more will see
Sohrab returning from the Tartar camp,
With spoils and honour, when the war is done.
But a dark rumour will be bruited up,
From tribe to tribe, until it reach her ear;
And then will that defenceless woman learn
That Sohrab will rejoice her sight no more;
But that in battle with a nameless foe,
By the far-distant Oxus, he is slain.'
He spoke; and as he ceased he wept aloud,
Thinking of her he left, and his own death.
He spoke; but Rustum listened, plunged in thought.
Nor did he yet believe it was his son
Who spoke, although he called back names he knew;
For he had had sure tidings that the babe,
Which was in Ader-baijan born to him,
Had been a puny girl, no boy at all:
So that sad mother sent him word, for fear
Rustum should take the boy, to train in arms;
And so he deemed that either Sohrab took,
By a false boast, the style of Rustum's son;
Or that men gave it him, to swell his fame.
So deemed he; yet he listened, plunged in thought;
And his soul set to grief, as the vast tide
Of the bright rocking ocean sets to shore
At the full moon: tears gathered in his eyes;
For he remembered his own early youth,

And all its bounding rapture; as, at dawn,
The shepherd from his mountain lodge descries
A far bright city, smitten by the sun,
Through many rolling clouds; – so Rustum saw
His youth; saw Sohrab's mother, in her bloom;
And that old King, her father, who loved well
His wandering guest, and gave him his fair child
With joy; and all the pleasant life they led,
They three, in that long-distant summer time –
The castle, and the dewy woods, and hunt
And hound, and morn on those delightful hills
In Ader-baijan. And he saw that youth,
Of age and looks to be his own dear son,
Piteous and lovely, lying on the sand,
Like some rich hyacinth, which by the scythe
Of an unskilful gardener has been cut,
Mowing the garden grass-plots near its bed,
And lies, a fragrant tower of purple bloom,
On the mown, dying grass; – so Sohrab lay,
Lovely in death, upon the common sand.
And Rustum gazed on him with grief, and said:
'O Sohrab, thou indeed art such a son
Whom Rustum, wert thou his, might well have loved!
Yet here thou errest, Sohrab, or else men
Have told thee false; – thou art not Rustum's son.
For Rustum had no son: one child he had –
But one – a girl: who with her mother now
Plies some light female task, nor dreams of us –
Of us she dreams not, nor of wounds, nor war.'
But Sohrab answered him in wrath; for now
The anguish of the deep-fixed spear grew fierce,
And he desired to draw forth the steel,
And let the blood flow free, and so to die;

But first he would convince his stubborn foe –
And, rising sternly on one arm, he said:
'Man, who art thou who dost deny my words?
Truth sits upon the lips of dying men,
And falsehood, while I lived, was far from mine.
I tell thee, pricked upon this arm I bear
That seal which Rustum to my mother gave,
That she might prick it on the babe she bore.'
He spoke; and all the blood left Rustum's cheeks,
And his knees tottered, and he smote his hand
Against his breast, his heavy mailed hand,
That the hard iron corslet clanked aloud;
And to his heart he pressed the other hand,
And in a hollow voice he spake, and said:
'Sohrab, that were a proof which could not lie.
If thou shew this, then art thou Rustum's son.'
Then, with weak hasty fingers, Sohrab loosed
His belt, and near the shoulder bared his arm,
And shewed a sign in faint vermilion points
Pricked; as a cunning workman, in Pekin,
Pricks with vermilion some clear porcelain vase,
An emperor's gift – at early morn he paints,
And all day long, and, when night comes, the lamp
Lights up his studious forehead and thin hands –
So delicately pricked the sign appeared
On Sohrab's arm, the sign of Rustum's seal.
It was that griffin, which of old reared Zal,
Rustum's great father, whom they left to die,
A helpless babe, among the mountain rocks.
Him that kind creature found, and reared, and loved –
Then Rustum took it for his glorious sign.
And Sohrab bared that figure on his arm,
And himself scanned it long with mournful eyes,

And then he touched it with his hand and said:
'How say'st thou? Is that sign the proper sign
Of Rustum's son, or of some other man's?'
He spoke: but Rustum gazed, and gazed, and stood
Speechless; and then he uttered one sharp cry –
O boy – thy father! – and his voice choked there.
And then a dark cloud passed before his eyes,
And his head swam, and he sank down to earth.
But Sohrab crawled to where he lay, and cast
His arms about his neck, and kissed his lips,
And with fond faltering fingers stroked his cheeks,
Trying to call him back to life: and life
Came back to Rustum, and he oped his eyes,
And they stood wide with horror; and he seized
In both his hands the dust which lay around,
And threw it on his head, and smirched his hair,
His hair, and face, and beard, and glittering arms:
And strong convulsive groanings shook his breast,
And his sobs choked him; and he clutched his sword,
To draw it, and for ever let life out.
But Sohrab saw his thought, and held his hands,
And with a soothing voice he spoke, and said:
'Father, forbear: for I but meet today
The doom that at my birth was written down
In Heaven, and thou art Heaven's unconscious hand.
Surely my heart cried out that it was thou,
When first I saw thee; and thy heart spoke too,
I know it: but fate trod those promptings down
Under its iron heel; fate, fate engaged
The strife and hurled me on my father's spear.
But let us speak no more of this: I find
My father; let me feel that I have found.
Come, sit beside me on this sand, and take

My head betwixt thy hands, and kiss my cheeks,
And wash them with thy tears, and say, *My son!*
Quick! quick! for numbered are my sands of life,
And swift; for like the lightning to this field
I came, and like the wind I go away –
Sudden, and swift, and like a passing wind.
But it was writ in Heaven that this should be.'
  So said he: and his voice released the heart
Of Rustum, and his tears broke forth; he cast
His arms round his son's neck, and wept aloud,
And kissed him. And awe fell on both the hosts
When they saw Rustum's grief: and Ruksh, the horse,
With his head bowing to the ground, and mane
Sweeping the dust, came near, and in mute woe
First to the one then to the other moved
His head, as if inquiring what their grief
Might mean; and from his dark compassionate eyes
The big warm tears rolled down, and caked the sand.
But Rustum chid him with stern voice, and said:
  'Ruksh, now thou grievest; but, O Ruksh, thy feet
Should then have rotted on their nimble joints,
When first they bore thy master to this field.'
  But Sohrab looked upon the horse and said:
'Is this then Ruksh? How often, in past days,
My mother told me of thee, thou brave steed!
My terrible father's terrible horse; and said,
That I should one day find thy lord and thee.
Come, let me lay my hand upon thy mane.
O Ruksh, thou art more fortunate than I;
For thou has gone where I shall never go,
And snuffed the breezes of my father's home.
And thou hast trod the sands of Seistan,
And seen the River of Helmund, and the Lake

Of Zirrah; and the aged Zal himself
Has often stroked thy neck, and given thee food,
Corn in a golden platter soaked with wine,
And said – *O Ruksh! bear Rustum well!* – but I
Have never known my grandsire's furrowed face,
Nor seen his lofty house in Seistan,
Nor slaked my thirst at the clear Helmund stream:
But lodged among my father's foes, and seen
Afrasiab's cities only, Samarcand,
Bokhara, and lone Khiva in the waste,
And the black Toorkmun tents; and only drunk
The desert rivers, Moorghab and Tejend,
Kohik, and where the Kalmuks feed their sheep,
The northern Sir; and this great Oxus stream –
The yellow Oxus, by whose brink I die.'
  And, with a heavy groan, Rustum replied:
'Oh that its waves were flowing over me!
Oh that I saw its grains of yellow silt
Roll tumbling in the current o'er my head!'
  And, with a grave mild voice, Sohrab replied:
'Desire not that, my father; thou must live.
For some are born to do great deeds, and live,
As some are born to be obscured, and die.
Do thou the deeds I die too young to do,
And reap a second glory in thine age.
Thou art my father, and thy gain is mine.
But come: thou seest this great host of men
Which follow me; I pray thee, slay not these:
Let me entreat for them: what have they done?
They followed me, my hope, my fame, my star.
Let them all cross the Oxus back in peace.
But me thou must bear hence, not send with them,
But carry me with thee to Seistan,

And place me on a bed, and mourn for me,
Thou, and the snow-haired Zal, and all thy friends.
And thou must lay me in that lovely earth,
And heap a stately mound above my bones,
And plant a far-seen pillar over all:
That so the passing horseman on the waste
May see my tomb a great way off, and say –
Sohrab, the mighty Rustum's son, lies there,
Whom his great father did in ignorance kill –
And I be not forgotten in my grave.'
  And, with a mournful voice, Rustum replied:
'Fear not; as thou hast said, Sohrab, my son,
So shall it be: for I will burn my tents,
And quit the host, and bear thee hence with me,
And carry thee away to Seistan,
And place thee on a bed, and mourn for thee,
With the snow-headed Zal, and all my friends.
And I will lay thee in that lovely earth,
And heap a stately mound above thy bones,
And plant a far-seen pillar over all:
And men shall not forget thee in thy grave.
And I will spare thy host: yea, let them go:
Let them all cross the Oxus back in peace.
What should I do with slaying any more?
For would that all whom I have ever slain
Might be once more alive; my bitterest foes,
And they who were called champions in their time,
And through whose death I won that fame I have;
And I were nothing but a common man,
A poor, mean soldier, and without renown,
So thou mightest live, too, my son, my son!
Or rather would that I, even I myself,
Might now be lying on this bloody sand,

Near death, and by an ignorant stroke of thine,
Not thou of mine; and I might die, not thou;
And I, not thou, be borne to Seistan;
And Zal might weep above my grave, not thine;
And say – *O son, I weep thee not too sore,*
For willingly, I know, thou met'st thine end.
But now in blood and battles was my youth,
And full of blood and battles is my age;
And I shall never end this life of blood.'
  Then, at the point of death, Sohrab replied:
'A life of blood indeed, thou dreadful man!
But thou shalt yet have peace; only not now;
Not yet: but thou shalt have it on that day,
When thou shalt sail in a high-masted ship,
Thou and the other peers of Kai Khosroo,
Returning home over the salt blue sea,
From laying thy dear master in his grave.'
  And Rustum gazed on Sohrab's face, and said:
'Soon be that day, my son, and deep that sea!
Till then, if fate so wills, let me endure.'
  He spoke; and Sohrab smiled on him, and took
The spear, and drew it from his side, and eased
His wound's imperious anguish: but the blood
Came welling from the open gash, and life
Flowed with the stream: all down his cold white side
The crimson torrent ran, dim now, and soiled,
Like the soiled tissue of white violets
Left, freshly gathered, on their native bank,
By romping children, whom their nurses call
From the hot fields at noon: his head drooped low,
His limbs grew slack; motionless, white, he lay –
White, with eyes closed; only when heavy gasps,
Deep, heavy gasps, quivering through all his frame,

Convulsed him back to life, he opened them,
And fixed them feebly on his father's face:
Till now all strength was ebbed, and from his limbs
Unwillingly the spirit fled away,
Regretting the warm mansion which it left,
And youth and bloom, and this delightful world.
So, on the bloody sand, Sohrab lay dead.
And the great Rustum drew his horseman's cloak
Down o'er his face, and sat by his dead son.
As those black granite pillars, once high-reared
By Jemshid in Persepolis, to bear
His house, now, mid their broken flights of steps
Lie prone, enormous, down the mountain side –
So in the sand lay Rustum by his son.
And night came down over the solemn waste,
And the two gazing hosts, and that sole pair,
And darkened all; and a cold fog, with night,
Crept from the Oxus. Soon a hum arose,
As of a great assembly loosed, and fires
Began to twinkle through the fog: for now
Both armies moved to camp, and took their meal:
The Persians took it on the open sands
Southward; the Tartars by the river marge:
And Rustum and his son were left alone.
But the majestic river floated on,
Out of the mist and hum of that low land,
Into the frosty starlight, and there moved,
Rejoicing, through the hushed Chorasmian waste,
Under the solitary moon: he flowed
Right for the Polar Star, past Orgunjè,
Brimming, and bright, and large: then sands begin
To hem his watery march, and dam his streams,
And split his currents; that for many a league

The shorn and parcelled Oxus strains along
Through beds of sand and matted rushy isles –
Oxus, forgetting the bright speed he had
In his high mountain cradle in Pamere,
A foiled circuitous wanderer: till at last
The longed-for dash of waves is heard, and wide
His luminous home of waters opens, bright
And tranquil, from whose floor the new-bathed stars
Emerge, and shine upon the Aral Sea.

Ticonderoga: A Legend of the West Highlands

Robert Louis Stevenson

First published in *Scribner's Magazine*,
December 1887

This is the tale of the man
  Who heard a word in the night
In the land of the heathery hills,
  In the days of the feud and the fight.
By the sides of the rainy sea,
  Where never a stranger came,
On the awful lips of the dead,
  He heard the outlandish name.
It sang in his sleeping ears,
  It hummed in his waking head:
The name – Ticonderoga,
  The utterance of the dead.

THE SAYING OF THE NAME

On the loch-sides of Appin,
  When the mist blew from the sea,
A Stewart stood with a Cameron:
  An angry man was he.
The blood beat in his ears,
  The blood ran hot to his head,
The mist blew from the sea,
  And there was the Cameron dead.
'O, what have I done to my friend,
  O, what have I done to mysel',

That he should be cold and dead,
And I in the danger of all?
'Nothing but danger about me,
Danger behind and before,
Death at wait in the heather
In Appin and Mamore,
Hate at all of the ferries
And death at each of the fords,
Camerons priming gunlocks
And Camerons sharpening swords.'

But this was a man of counsel,
This was a man of a score,
There dwelt no pawkier Stewart
In Appin or Mamore.
He looked on the blowing mist,
He looked on the awful dead,
And there came a smile on his face
And there slipped a thought in his head.

Out over cairn and moss,
Out over scrog and scaur,
He ran as runs the clansman
That bears the cross of war.
His heart beat in his body,
His hair clove to his face,
When he came at last in the gloaming
To the dead man's brother's place.
The east was white with the moon,
The west with the sun was red,
And there, in the house-doorway,
Stood the brother of the dead.

'I have slain a man to my danger,
  I have slain a man to my death,
I put my soul in your hands,'
  The panting Stewart saith.
'I lay it bare in your hands,
  For I know your hands are leal;
And be you my targe and bulwark
  From the bullet and the steel.'

Then up and spoke the Cameron,
  And gave him his hand again:
'There shall never a man in Scotland
  Set faith in me in vain;
And whatever man you have slaughtered,
  Of whatever name or line,
By my sword and yonder mountain,
  I make your quarrel mine.
I bid you in to my fireside,
  I share with you house and hall;
It stands upon my honour
  To see you safe from all.'

It fell in the time of midnight,
  When the fox barked in the den,
And the plaids were over the faces
  In all the houses of men,
That as the living Cameron
  Lay sleepless on his bed,
Out of the night and the other world
  Came in to him the dead.

'My blood is on the heather,
  My bones are on the hill;

There is joy in the home of ravens
  That the young shall eat their fill.
My blood is poured in the dust,
  My soul is spilled in the air;
And the man that has undone me
  Sleeps in my brother's care.'

'I'm wae for your death, my brother,
  But if all of my house were dead,
I couldnae withdraw the plighted hand
Nor break the word once said.'

'O, what shall I say to our father,
  In the place to which I fare?
O, what shall I say to our mother,
  Who greets to see me there?
And to all the kindly Camerons
  That have lived and died long-syne –
Is this the word you send them,
  Fause-hearted brother mine?'

'It's neither fear nor duty,
  It's neither quick nor dead
Shall gar me withdraw the plighted hand,
  Or break the word once said.'

Thrice in the time of midnight,
  When the fox barked in the den,
And the plaids were over the faces
  In all the houses of men,
Thrice as the living Cameron
  Lay sleepless on his bed,
Out of the night and the other world

Came in to him the dead,
And cried to him for vengeance
On the man that laid him low;
And thrice the living Cameron
Told the dead Cameron, no.

'Thrice have you seen me, brother,
But now shall see me no more,
Till you meet your angry fathers
Upon the farther shore.
Thrice have I spoken, and now,
Before the cock be heard,
I take my leave for ever
With the naming of a word.
It shall sing in your sleeping ears,
It shall hum in your waking head,
The name – Ticonderoga,
And the warning of the dead.'

Now when the night was over
And the time of people's fears,
The Cameron walked abroad,
And the word was in his ears.
'Many a name I know,
But never a name like this;
O, where shall I find a skilly man
Shall tell me what it is?'
With many a man he counselled
Of high and low degree,
With the herdsmen on the mountains
And the fishers of the sea.
And he came and went unweary,
And read the books of yore,

And the runes that were written of old
  On stones upon the moor.
And many a name he was told,
  But never the name of his fears –
Never, in east or west,
  The name that rang in his ears:
Names of men and of clans;
  Names for the grass and the tree,
For the smallest tarn in the mountains,
  The smallest reef in the sea:
Names for the high and low
  The names of the craig and the flat;
But in all the land of Scotland,
  Never a name like that.

THE SEEKING OF THE NAME

And now there was speech in the south,
  And a man of the south that was wise,
A periwigged lord of London,
  Called on the clans to rise.
And the riders rode, and the summons
  Came to the western shore,
To the land of the sea and the heather,
  To Appin and Mamore.
It called on all to gather
  From every scrog and scaur,
That loved their father's tartan
  And the ancient game of war.
And down the watery valley
  And up the windy hill,
Once more, as in the olden,
  The pipes were sounding shrill.
Again in highland sunshine

The naked steel was bright;
And the lads, once more in tartan,
Went forth again to fight.

'O, why should I dwell here
With a weird upon my life,
When the clansmen shout for battle
And the war-swords clash in strife?
I cannae joy at feast,
I cannae sleep in bed,
For the wonder of the word
And the warning of the dead.
It sings in my sleeping ears,
It hums in my waking head,
The name – Ticonderoga,
The utterance of the dead.
Then up, and with the fighting men
To march away from here,
Till the cry of the great war-pipe
Shall drown it in my ear!'

Where flew King George's ensign
The plaided soldiers went:
They drew the sword in Germany,
In Flanders pitched the tent.
The bells of foreign cities
Rang far across the plain:
They passed the happy Rhine,
They drank the rapid Main.
Through Asiatic jungles
The Tartans filed their way,
And the neighing of the war-pipes
Struck terror in Cathay.

'Many a name have I heard,' he thought,
 'In all the tongues of men,
Full many a name both here and there,
 Full many both now and then.
When I was at home in my father's house
 In the land of the naked knee,
Between the eagles that fly in the lift
 And the herrings that swim in the sea,
And now that I am a captain-man
 With a braw cockade in my hat –
Many a name have I heard,' he thought,
 'But never a name like that.'

THE PLACE OF THE NAME

There fell a war in a woody place,
 Lay far across the sea,
A war of the march in the mirk midnight
 And the shot from behind the tree,
The shaven head and the painted face,
 The silent foot in the wood,
In a land of a strange, outlandish tongue
 That was hard to be understood.

It fell about the gloaming,
 The general stood with his staff,
He stood and he looked east and west
 With little mind to laugh.
'Far have I been and much have I seen,
 And kent both gain and loss,
But here we have woods on every hand
 And a kittle water to cross.
Far have I been and much have I seen,
 But never the beat of this;

And there's one must go down to that waterside
To see how deep it is.'

It fell in the dusk of the night
When unco things betide,
The skilly captain, the Cameron,
Went down to that waterside.
Canny and soft the captain went;
And a man of the woody land,
With the shaven head and the painted face,
Went down at his right hand.
It fell in the quiet night,
There was never a sound to ken;
But all the woods to the right and the left
Lay filled with the painted men.

'Far have I been and much have I seen,
Both as a man and boy,
But never have I set forth a foot
On so perilous an employ.'
It fell in the dusk of the night
When unco things betide,
That he was aware of a captain-man
Drew near to the waterside.
He was aware of his coming
Down in the gloaming alone;
And he looked in the face of the man,
And lo! the face was his own.
'This is my weird,' he said,
'And now I ken the worst;
For many shall fall with the morn,
But I shall fall with the first.
O, you of the outland tongue,

You of the painted face,
This is the place of my death;
Can you tell me the name of the place?'

'Since the Frenchmen have been here
They have called it Sault-Marie;
But that is a name for priests,
And not for you and me.
It went by another word,'
Quoth he of the shaven head:
'It was called Ticonderoga
In the days of the great dead.'

And it fell on the morrow's morning,
In the fiercest of the fight,
That the Cameron bit the dust
As he foretold at night;
And far from the hills of heather
Far from the isles of the sea,
He sleeps in the place of the name
As it was doomed to be.